# Blaine's Law

**Center Point
Large Print**

**This Large Print Book carries the
Seal of Approval of N.A.V.H.**

ॐ श्री गणेशाय नमः

# Blaine's Law

## Carter Travis Young

**Center Point Publishing**
Thorndike, Maine

This Center Point Large Print edition
is published in the year 2002 by arrangement with
Golden West Literary Agency.

The text of this Large Print edition is unabridged.
In other aspects, this book may vary from the original
edition. Printed in Thailand. Set in 16-point
Times New Roman type by Bill Coskrey.

ISBN 1-58547-198-4

Library of Congress Cataloging-in-Publication Data.

Young, Carter Travis.
   Blaine's law / Carter Travis Young.--Center Point large print ed.
     p. cm.
   ISBN 1-58547-198-4 (lib. bdg. : alk. paper)
    1. Large type books.  I. Title.

PS3575.O7 B57 2002
813'.54--dc21
                                       2002019131

# ONE

Cullom Blaine rode out of a canyon blackness that was like a massive weight pressing against him on both sides, and into a lingering purple dusk. At the far edge of a sparsely set table below him, marked by the wriggling track of a small creek, a campfire danced, its light a feeble flicker in the thickening gloom.

Fire. Blaine felt his belly twist. There was a burning sensation in his middle, as if that distant glow found an answering flame in his gut.

There was also tension like a hand between his shoulder blades. He lifted his wide, heavy shoulders as if to shrug off the feeling. He knew that he wouldn't find Lem Seevers straddle-legged before that fire. There would be only two men . . . and three horses. For some time he had known that the third horse carried no weight.

He rode down a long slope, not hurrying now, accepting the fact of darkness and the end of the day's trail as a patient man will.

Cullom Blaine had learned patience this past year. Learned to rein the wildness of his yearling hatred. Learned to sift the garrulous dust of rumor and conversation for stray glints of worth to him. Learned to conserve his anger lest he spend its force too soon, before he had found them all, the men he hunted.

He walked his buckskin across the open, letting the two men camped beside the creek hear him from a long way off, giving them time to judge the openness of his approach. Some men—jittery or guilty—reacted recklessly when they were surprised. Blaine had no reason to provoke that recklessness in the two whose tracks had brought him to this meeting.

Not yet.

They were waiting for him when he rode up to the fire, the clap of the buckskin's hoofs loud in the stillness of an August night that was turning pleasantly cool. Blaine could feel the light breeze drying the big sweat circle in the middle of his back. One of the men was standing, a tall youngster with round shoulders and a protruding neck and head. The other, a huge man drowning in his own fat, remained squatting before the fire, a tin cup of coffee lost in the black-haired nest of his hand.

"Howdy," Blaine said easily. "Smelled that coffee a mile back. It pulled me in like a calf on a rope."

"Fall off and cool your saddle," the big man rumbled. He gestured with his lost cup. "There's plenty coffee."

The thinner, younger man showed considerable interest in Blaine and his horse, noting the darkness of sweat on the buckskin and the heavy coating of trail dust on both horse and rider, some of which Blaine slapped off his clothes with his nearly shapeless hat before he came to the fire.

Blaine accepted beans with his coffee. If he stayed he had bacon to share for the morning to pay his way, not that men begrudged a few beans on the trail. There was some desultory talk about the day's heat. The two men—the lanky kid was Archer, the big hairy man Curly—were cowhands returning south after a long cattle drive that started up the Western Trail in late spring. A few weeks before, at the end of the drive, they had had three months' wages scorching their pockets. Now both men were broke. They didn't seem

6

much concerned.

"Thin likker and fat women," Archer declared with an air of boasting. "They took it all."

"Generally do," Blaine commented.

The mood was easy, and the other men relaxed, when Blaine asked about Lem Seevers. Curly blinked at him slowly, his eyelids raising and lowering like shutters among the folds of his broad face. Young Archer sat up, head poking forward aggressively. He had pop-eyes that bulged when he showed interest, as he did now.

"Seevers?" He grinned for no reason Blaine could see. "What makes you think we'd know?"

"I thought you might."

"You thought we might, huh? Well, you got another think comin', mister."

The sandy-haired stranger who faced Archer across the campfire, lounging carelessly on the end of his spine, wasn't big enough or mean enough in the face to make a cocky youngster think twice. Blaine was six feet tall but didn't look it. You had to look closely to see just how powerful those wide shoulders were, and how deep the chest. His hips and waist were lean, encased in faded jeans that had shrunk to a snug fit. His sun-darkened face was almost gaunt, bringing a strongly bridged nose and high cheekbones into prominence. His brown eyes, their irises flecked with an emerald green, were bright as jewels in that dark face. His shirt was old and worn, bleached nearly white, his leather vest and boots cracked and poor-mouthed by the dust they carried. Aside from his eyes, the red bandanna around his neck was the only clear mark of color on him, and it owed some of its brightness to the fact that he had recently wrung it out in water and used it to bathe his neck and face. The gaze of his arresting eyes, like the easy rumble of his voice, was at the moment deceptively mild.

Yet an older man, or a more cautious one like Curly, saw other things. There was a rock steadiness to the man. His face was not mean, but it had no softness about it at all, no twinkle to temper the steady bore of those green-flecked brown eyes, no lifting corner to ease the tight line of his lips, which closed like the two planes of a vise. There was something unyielding in him, but it was not a quality for show, an arrogance or belligerence intended to give him an edge over a less confident man. It was simply there, like the solidity of a rock that hasn't moved for generations of winds and rains and seasonal storms.

And there was something else: a coldness. He looked as if he felt no emotion at all, as if he didn't care if the young cowhand answered him easy or hard. He would learn what he wanted to know in the end, one way or another, and it didn't much matter to him how it had to be.

Blaine said, "You were riding with him."

"Is that a fact now?" Archer grinned at his companion, who frowned back. "And how would you know that, Mr. Blaine?"

"I been followin' you."

The young waddie pushed to his feet. Curly continued to blink slowly, not moving. That was a lot of weight to move unnecessarily, Blaine thought. Curly must have packed two hundred and fifty pounds.

"I don't like bein' followed!" Archer snapped.

"Don't blame you," Blaine said easily. "It wasn't your tracks I was interested in, it's this fellow Seevers I asked

8

you about. You just happened to fall in with him."

"We din't fall in with nobody!"

Archer was angry now, or he was parading ruffled feathers as he had paraded his liking for hard liquor and soft women. Or he was testing himself as much as he challenged Blaine, the way a youngster will. And maybe he mistook the quiet way Blaine spoke for diffidence.

"He was on a pinto. Joined up with you a couple days north of Chadbourne. Likely just rode in the way I did for coffee. Man ain't much to look at, but that pinto has brown ears coming out of white and a kind of white shield across his chest."

"I told you we din't ride with nobody. You callin' me a liar?"

Blaine eyed him without change of expression, feeling neither regret nor pleasure over what was coming. It always seemed to happen. Maybe it was something in him that men felt or sensed, something stubborn and dangerous that jolted them and awakened fear . . . and with that fear an answering stubbornness, an unwillingness to admit the fear.

No matter. What would happen would happen.

But he needed to know about Seevers.

Blaine had picked up the trail in Fort Worth, where a man answering to the name of Seevers had bought a ticket for Weatherford. Blaine had done the same.

He might have lost the trail right there but for a talkative conductor. Yes, he remembered a Mr. Seevers, gentleman bound for Weatherford. A little the worse for wear, Mr. Seevers was, but a man who wasn't used to trains could get that way, affected by the smoke and the noise and worst of all the bouncing gait of the train along the iron rails. He never could understand how a man used to riding a horse—Mr. Seevers looked like he would be more at home in the saddle—could get sick traveling in luxury on a train, but some did. Mr. Seevers—

"Did he get off at Weatherford?" Blaine was not even sure why he asked the question. He was only half listening, thinking ahead.

Well, that's why the conductor remembered Mr. Seevers. Him being so surly and all, and then being sick. He had to send Seevers to the back of the caboose so he could be sick there in peace, but a man enjoying his cigar on the back platform had got into a quarrel with Mr. Seevers over the cigar, whose smell and smoke seemed to make Mr. Seevers feel worse. The conductor had never seen such a bad case of train sickness, and he'd been with the railroad for nearly ten years—not all of that in this godforsaken wasteland, of course.

So he had noticed that Mr. Seevers did not get off at Weatherford, and he remembered his ticket being for Weatherford. Had to sell him another ticket to Palo Pinto, which was just west of the point where the tracks crossed the Brazos, and where Mr. Seevers, looking very pale and on unsteady legs, actually disembarked from the train.

By then Blaine was wide-awake, listening and grateful. He asked a few more questions but he had learned everything useful the conductor had to tell him. A few prodding questions about Seevers' appearance produced only the news that he was "no bigger than average," had dark hair and beard in need of a trim, undistinguished clothes, and "a surly manner." The description would have fit more travelers than not.

In Palo Pinto, Seevers had turned into "Earl Smith," and there he had purchased a pinto with distinctive chest markings and "brown ears out of a white field." Blaine judged rightly that he would find it easier to track the pinto than the man, who seemed to have no visible markings to make him memorable.

The trail of the pinto and its nondescript rider had led Blaine northwest across the Clear Fork of the Brazos, then a long loop around some forbidding buttes to Fort Griffin. There the pinto's owner had become "John Soames." He had ridden south, following Red Creek and the old Overland Mail Route. Two days out of Fort Griffin he had come upon the camp of two other men. From that campsite there had been three sets of tracks for Blaine to follow. One set of hoofprints sank deep enough into the sandy ground to suggest that the rider was a big heavy man. The other new set included an easily read chip in one of the shoes. The tracks were recent, and Blaine had felt that he was closing in on Lem Seevers.

He sniffed those tracks into Fort Chadbourne. There a hostler remembered the big man and his companions passing through, but they hadn't stayed long enough to sleep. One of the men was surly and impatient, reluctant to wait for a cracked shoe to be replaced. Blaine was less than twenty-four hours behind them.

The three sets of tracks led south, one identified by the chipped shoe, the other by the weight of the rider. The other was a newly shod horse, and Blaine figured the hostler had simply neglected to mention fitting new shoes all around.

He slept only a few hours that night. When he picked up

the trail again in the first light he confirmed a suspicion that had made his brief stop restless. The freshly shod horse was not the pinto Lem Seevers had been riding. Its stride was longer, lighter.

Blaine was tempted to turn back, but he had a hunch that Seevers might have been clever enough to switch mounts with a stranger . . . if he knew that Blaine was close to clipping his heels.

He had guessed wrong. He still didn't know what Seevers looked like, but he knew that neither Archer nor Curly was the man he hunted.

"You're the one that's callin' names," Blaine said. "Why don't you just sit down, son."

"Damn you—"

"Shut up, Billy," Curly broke in. "Do like he says. Sit down."

"Hell you say!" Archer glared at Curly, as if he welcomed the excuse to focus his anger there.

Curly ignored him, gazing speculatively at Blaine. "You must have a powerful good reason for doggin' this man you call Seevers."

"Good enough."

Curly blinked, his small eyes disappearing behind heavy curtains, then peering out again. "Blaine," he murmured. "Seems to me like I heard of one Blaine."

Blaine said nothing. Archer, ignored, had stalked away from the fire, but interest pulled him back. "Who was he? A dust chaser like this one?"

Blaine looked at him. "I had a bell once," he said. "Dinner bell, it was, had a loose clapper. Every time the wind would come up that clapper would start makin' a racket, like it was time to quit work. I had to jerk that clapper out."

Archer was slow to read Blaine's meaning, but when he did he pulled taut as a bowstring. "You wanta try it on this here bell, mister? I'll give you some noise to make your head ring!"

He was quivering, and his hand pawed the air nervously at his side, just above the butt of a holstered Colt. It had happened too suddenly and there had been no way to turn it aside. Blaine saw that trouble was the only way he could discover what he sought. Curly seemed a reasonable enough hombre, but the young goose-necked kid had been spoiling for trouble ever since Blaine rode in. He wondered why, and asked himself belatedly if it could have anything to do with Seevers, if there was a link between Seevers and Archer that he hadn't guessed.

"Whatcha waitin' for, Mr. Blaine? Is it 'cause I'm showin' you my face? What I hear, you're good at lookin' down the barrel at a man's spine."

Blaine nodded to himself, understanding, confirming a hunch that Lem Seevers now knew that Blaine was on his trail and not far behind. God knew what story he had told the impressionable and hot-tempered Billy Archer. Whatever, it was likely to get someone killed.

Blaine knew better than most men that the law in the West was often what you made it. If a man thought himself insulted, he could call another down in a fair fight and no law would try to punish him, or if it did no jury would convict the survivor. There might be more scoundrels and blackguards here in Texas than could be found all along the entire Atlantic seaboard, but what a man might be didn't weigh any more than what he might have done in another life somewhere. Here he had a right to his good name, even if it was one he had chosen recently. He had absolute claim to the horse that carried his saddle and the cattle that carried his brand, and he could defend them any way he had to without being faulted. He could defend them, and his house, and his woman. And when they were taken from him, as Blaine's had been, he sought his own sudden justice.

He had no quarrel with Billy Archer, but the kid had said things that couldn't be ignored.

Blaine eased his weight onto his left side. "Like I said, son, you got a loose clapper."

He saw Curly's move first, a rippling of mounds of flesh that transformed itself with startling speed into the gleam of gun metal, dark red in the firelight. Blaine rolled and kicked the coffeepot into the fat man's face.

By then Archer was clearing leather. Blaine didn't hesitate. He wanted Archer alive long enough to talk. Curly was screaming and cursing as the scalding coffee from the fire spilled over him. Blaine reversed his roll, sliding toward the fire as Archer jerked his Colt out and squeezed off a shot too hastily. Blaine used both hands as a scoop to pick up sand and dust, fire ashes and burning embers, and flung the pile directly at Archer.

The kid screamed. He dropped his gun as he pawed at live flames leaping over his shirt front. Blaine whirled, his own gun jumping into his hand. Curly was on his hands and knees, one side of his beefy face red as raw meat from the hot liquid which had burned it, his hairy hand groping like a fat spider for the gun he had lost.

"Don't!" Blaine lashed out. When Curly's hand pulled back he said, "It's not worth it. Not for the likes of Seevers. He ain't worth dyin' for."

With a choked cry of rage Archer jumped him. Blaine moved only a single step, economically, turning his body to evade the tall youth's wild lunge. His right hand moved in a short, chopping arc. The barrel of his Single Action Army Colt, a solid eight and a half inches long, thunked against Archer's skull. The kid fell into him, sagging. Blaine stepped clear, his gun once again covering Curly's ample middle as Archer slid to the ground.

The big man made no further move. Yes, he was a reasonable man, Blaine thought.

Archer half sprawled over the blackened remains of the fire. Blaine holstered his Colt and dragged the youngster away from the hot ashes. He put out some glowing ash that was burning Archer's shirt and flicked the live coals off him. The fire was a lost cause and Blaine gave no thought to rescuing what was left of it. No one was hungry now and he guessed that Curly had had enough coffee. There was also a dense congregation of stars to light the sky and people the empty land.

While they waited for Archer to wake up, Blaine asked Curly about Seevers. The fat man hadn't known the stranger who had joined them south of Fort Griffin by that name—he was still calling himself Soames—but he was certain that Seevers, if such he was, had remained behind at Chadbourne when Curly and Archer pulled out.

"I looked for that pinto," Blaine said. "It wasn't there."

"Maybe you'll have to ask him," Curly said, nodding toward Archer, who was beginning to moan and stir about, showing signs of recovery. "He and Soames hit it off, seemed like. They talked some. I didn't much taken notice."

When Archer woke, groaning over some burns on his cheek and hands, he shook memory alive as his eyes found Blaine studying him. He began to curse Blaine, dragging up every vile name he could think of. Blaine waited for the venom to spend itself, unmoved. Archer wasn't very inventive, he thought, for a Texian.

"You like to flap your tongue," Blaine said when Archer fell silent. "Now you're gonna talk about Seevers, or Soames, if that's what he called himself to you."

"Go to hell."

"Soon enough," Blaine said pleasantly.

He slapped Archer across the side of the face with his open palm. It looked like a light blow but it wasn't. It rocked Archer's head and made his eyes water. "You can't make me—"

"I can," Blaine said.

The second slap, like the first, traveled no more than a few inches, but was even harder. It made a sharp crack like dry kindling broken across a man's knee. Archer had a fresh burn on that cheek, already blistering, and the blow caused the tender flesh to sting painfully. He flinched away from the third punishing slap, crying out, "All right! Lemme alone."

Blaine waited for the kid to regain his composure. He would talk more freely when he was able to feel less ashamed. Blaine didn't much like what he was doing, but he didn't regret it either. All he wanted was information. Archer had made it trouble.

"This fellow Soames. He told you I back-shot someone?"

"Yeah."

"He's a liar." Blaine did not feel it necessary to explain further. "What happened to his horse?"

Archer hesitated. He looked as if he didn't want to answer the question but he cared even less for Blaine to start hitting him again. There was hate in his pale eyes. "He was at Fort Chadbourne," the young man said finally, the words sullen and reluctant. "You just looked right at him and went by."

"How would that be?"

"Soames stained him dark so's you wouldn't notice him if you had a description. He was gonna use pitch and grease and whatever he could get hold of. I never seen it. We took out."

Blaine frowned. The stables were under roof, dark to begin with. It would have been easy for a man coming in out of the sun to overlook unnatural darkening in a horse's coat. Especially a careless or a hasty man, he thought with disgust, looking for one thing only, those distinctive markings on the pinto.

"So you took out leading a third horse. Whose idea was that, Soames's? So's I'd think he was still with you? He pay for that horse, did he?"

"I told you all I'm gonna tell."

Blaine saw that Archer was trying to regain some pride by taking a belated stand. It didn't matter. Blaine already had all the important answers he was likely to get. Seevers had had to do something to buy loyalty that would last beyond sunset. The third horse explained it.

"Just one other thing . . ." Blaine murmured.

His right hand suddenly became a fist. It moved only seven or eight inches, but this time the blow was not a slap. It snapped Archer's head back with an audible clicking of jaws, hair flying out from his head. The young waddie slumped to the ground.

Blaine rose. He was going to have to backtrack and that meant no time for sleep. Already Seevers had gained too much of a jump.

"When he wakes up you tell him," Blaine said. "Tell him he better quit callin' names till he's old enough to back it up."

Curly had not stirred when Blaine flattened his partner. He sighed heavily. "He ain't a bad kid."

"He won't live to be a worse one."

After Blaine had gone Curly stared somberly for a while at Archer. Then he pushed himself up—when he wasn't in a hurry it seemed a great effort for him to heave his bulk around—and found his canteen. He took a short swallow, holding it thoughtfully in his mouth for a bit, staring into the darkness after Blaine. Then he upended the canteen, pouring its contents over Archer's face and neck.

The kid came awake sputtering and swinging. Curly placed a boot on his chest and held him down. Archer's thrashings stopped abruptly.

"Where is he?" he demanded, panting with anger. "Where is the son of a bitch?"

"Gone," Curly said curtly. "Lucky for you, I reckon."

"Hell you say."

Archer rose to his feet and prowled the circle of the

campsite, his head thrust forward, eyes glaring off into the darkness. His legs were still a little wobbly from that single punch, or from the earlier blow on the head with the gun barrel.

Finally he returned to his saddlebags and rummaged blindly in one of the pockets until he found what he wanted. He dragged out a bottle of white mule, uncorked it with his teeth, spat out the cork, and tilted the bottle. He brought it down, choking and gasping. Curly grinned at the performance, but he said nothing. Archer had a quick temper, and his pride had been bruised as badly as his jaw this night.

Curly hadn't known about the bottle. Neither he nor Archer had had enough silver left to buy it. Seevers must have thrown the bottle in with the horse as part of the bargain, Curly thought. It was short pay for bucking that man Blaine.

Archer took another pull at the bottle before he handed it across to Curly. "Son of a bitch," he repeated. "It ain't over. We'll tangle again."

"You better hope not," Curly said. The mule was well named, with a kick to match.

"Yeah? I notice you din't do nothin' to ruffle him."

Curly ignored the caustic comment. "I din't owe nothin' to that Soames, or Seevers. That was your own idea and a damn fool one. You keep stickin' your nose into other men's arguments, you'll keep gettin' it chopped off."

Archer scowled, started a retort, swallowed it. "Who is this Blaine? I din't see no badge. You said you heard tell of him."

Curly nodded slowly. "Somewheres. He ain't the law.

What I remember, he's a hunter. Seevers must be one of the men he's huntin'. I hear he's caught up with a few."

"What for? A man don't hunt without a reason."

"I don't know the whole of it." Curly thought of Blaine, and of the quality he had sensed in the man, a core of purpose so unyielding that nothing would bend it while the man still drew breath. He took another drink and reluctantly handed the bottle back. That white poison burned all the way down, hot enough to track. "It must've been somethin' bad. Real bad." He regarded his young sidekick speculatively. Archer's jaw was already swollen on the left side where Blaine's fist had exploded. "Be glad you're out of it, son. Just be glad you wasn't in the way when that son of a bitch caught up with your friend Soames."

## TWO

At the top of the pass Lem Seevers tied the pinto loosely to the blasted trunk of a dead tree. Nothing lived in that barren terrain. The pinto, which had a strange appearance from the unnatural dye around his head and chest, plain enough in the bright sunlight, poked his nose at Seevers and nickered softly, but Seevers turned away, too nervous and impatient to search for grass or such edible leaves as this increasingly desolate country offered.

He left the horse, which had been laboring up the last part of the climb, and clambered over the rocks that formed the broken shoulder on the right side of the trail. After a short distance he stumbled onto a narrow animal path, an old sheep trail by the look of it. It led him on a steep climb that brought him quickly to the rimrock lookout he had spotted from below, far down the pass.

Foolishly he stood erect as he rose to the natural lookout, in his eagerness forgetting that he skylined himself all too clearly. No man could know what eyes might be watching him, or alert for any movement against a far rim. That tree-less plain to the west, all coarse grass and sand, was Comanche and Kiowa country, stretching for hundreds of miles to the north through the Indian Territory. And even without that threat a man on the run knew better than to call attention to himself. Unless, like Seevers, he was exhausted, pushed to his limit or beyond.

The heat on that high slab at midday was brutal, radiating from the rocks below and beating down on him from an enormous copper kettle of sky above, whose morning blue had turned white and then yellow with the heat haze. The heat rose from the vast prairie he overlooked in shim-mering waves, distorting objects and distances. The whole vista might have been a mirage, it looked so murky and unreal. Southwest were razor-backed mountains, and at their feet, visible to him for the first time, were the wrig-gling tributaries of the Colorado River that ran eastward for a spell before it dipped south and eventually ran into the Gulf of Mexico, effectively cutting Texas in half. In that southerly direction, and especially eastward where there was plentiful water, were good ranch lands. The bleak plain to the west was far less hospitable, a barren desert from which starkly shaped towers and cathedrals thrust their stone spires and bulwarks.

And to the north, visible for fifty miles or more from this height, was the trail Seevers had followed.

Then, straining, his bloodshot eyes squinting to red slits,

he saw it: a small plume of dust that thinned out and mush-roomed as it rose into the heat waves until it was lost in the general haze.

Damn him! Goddamn him!

Lem Seevers dropped to his knees, for a moment heed-less of the searing heat of the rock on which he knelt. He was close to blubbering, near collapse. The endless days and weeks of relentless pursuit—they had run together, those days, no longer a measure of time, one indistinct from the other—had chipped away at his cool arrogance, changing him, weakening him, making him doubt himself and fear his pursuer. My God, wasn't he human? Didn't he ever have to stop to rest?

Ordinarily Lem Seevers was not a man to run from anyone or anything. There were notches on his gun butt to prove it, the first one carved when he was eighteen years old. At first he had told himself that he ran from the law, not from one angry man. After all, the Clancy brothers and Wes Hannifin had been caught and tried, sent to the Texas Penitentiary. Seevers couldn't know what names they might have traded to save their necks. If they hadn't made a bargain, why hadn't they stretched ropes? Seevers had to figure that he might be wanted, even though he had seen no poster with his name. That was why, after leaving Fort Worth, he had changed his name.

But after a while he knew that it wasn't the law he ran from. The law gave up after a while. There were always new crimes, a fresh hue and cry, another robbery or another killing. Violence and death were not rare incidents on the frontier. The law couldn't hold fresh the memory and the rage over one woman's dying.

Blaine could, and did.

And the word had come, as such news did, that Abe Still-well was dead—Abe with his roaring life and his quick guns, feared even by the Clancy brothers, chopped down in the street up in Fort Smith, by a granite-hard scourge of a man who had taken one of Abe's bullets without going down, and had shot back to kill. A man called Blaine.

First Abe Stillwell. Then Brownie, holed up on the far side of Texas, a world away from Fort Smith, hiding out below the border and sneaking up to El Paso when he knew it was safe. Sneaking into a darkened crib and suddenly feeling iron hands close around his throat.

And now Seevers.

No wonder he ran. There was something inhuman about this man Blaine, and something equally terrible in the guilt Lem Seevers felt—the guilt Stillwell and Brownie had also carried, just as Tom and Art Clancy and Wes Hannifin did over there in the Huntsville prison, wasting away behind thick walls, but safe.

It was the woman. They should have buried her, and maybe buried some of Blaine's fury with her. That had been Wes's idea, boarding her up in the house, still alive after all they had done to her. Tom and Art had thought it was funny, and Abe Stillwell had roared with laughter when she started to beg. Seevers hadn't liked that part of it, nor the sweaty grin on Wes Hannifin's skull face. He'd been glad to ride away until he could no longer hear the woman's shrill pleading.

Sure, he'd taken his pleasure of her like the others. Why not? It was her last chance, wasn't it? You couldn't tell him that a woman didn't take some enjoyment out of it, no matter if she cried rape afterward. And the Blaine woman was as good as dead then, they all knew that. She couldn't be left to point a finger at each of them. That would have been like fitting the noose around their own necks.

Seevers rose to his feet, swaying from the heat and from exhaustion. But his momentary despair, born of that terrible fatigue, was slipping away, replaced by rage. Let Blaine follow! It would do him no good. He was too far behind now. He'd never catch Seevers before he reached the sanctuary that lay among those sawtoothed mountains to the southwest.

Price's Landing. Seevers had never been there, but he had heard enough about the hideout. He'd known men who had been there, and there might even be some there now he could call friend, outlaws of his own stripe.

Blaine couldn't follow him there. And if he did he would ride against fifty guns instead of one.

Let him come, Seevers thought as he slid and stumbled down the narrow sheep trail toward his waiting, hungry horse. Let the bastard come and buck Sam Price's guns!

# THREE

Cullom Blaine made noon camp in the shade of a small grove of box elder, within sight of the Red Fork of the Colorado. There was little enough shade in this sun-blasted land, little relief from the punishing heat during the day. A man going a long way took advantage of it when he could, unless he was nudged by panic.

Like Seevers. He'd kill that pinto if he kept on the way he was going. Blaine was a little surprised the horse hadn't given out on him before this.

Still, that trick at Chadbourne had bought Seevers the time he needed. Blaine had had to double back and search for his trail all over again. By the time he found it Seevers was as much as two days' ride ahead of him. Blaine had closed the gap again—to less than a day, he judged—but not fast enough, if his guess was correct about where Seevers' tracks were leading now.

Blaine had been a long time in the saddle. He knew that he lost no ground by resting during the midday heat, as he did now, while Seevers punished himself and his horse. Later, while Blaine rode easily through the cool of evening and into darkness, Seevers generally collapsed by a cold camp and stayed longer than necessary, sleeping an hour longer than a man needed to to keep going. Randy, Blaine's buckskin, was still strong, with plenty of run in reserve, the result of consideration that had practical as well as humanitarian benefits; Seevers' dyed pinto had to be laboring. And Blaine himself was fresher. He could choose his time and place to rest. He could build a fire for his coffee and bacon or beans, not caring if Seevers was close enough to see it. If he was, that would only keep the panic nudging him, and fear wore a man down as much as anything.

But with all that Seevers could still win this hand. He was not a smart man—no one but a fool would skyline himself in country like this, where the naked eye could pick out a moving speck on rimrock over immeasurable distances— but he was cunning, and he had the cunning man's instinct for survival.

Seevers had had to make a choice. He could have headed east, and if he had he would soon have been able to lose his tracks for a while in that more settled ranch country. That way he could have thrown Blaine completely off his trail, and gained a longer run for himself. Why hadn't he? Blaine's guess was that he had acted out of fear. That way, even among people, Seevers would have been alone, and he never would have been able to stop running. Seevers wanted company of his own kind. He had turned southwest toward the only place he could find it.

By nightfall Seevers would be over the visible range of hills. Blaine had only hearsay to go on after that, but he figured that another day or two of hard riding would bring Lem Seevers to Price's Landing. If that guess was accurate, Blaine no longer had much hope of intercepting him. Seevers might be able to ride that pinto into the ground, get off and walk the rest of the way before Blaine could catch up. Blaine understood this, accepted it, without disappointment, without emotion of any kind.

Price's Landing, he thought, the midday heat lying heavy on his lids even in the shade. Among so many thieves a cowardly thief could find courage.

The sun burned his cheek, awakening him. It slanted lower, under the branches of the trees, edging the patch of shadow away from the spot where Blaine lay. Hot as an iron, Blaine thought; hot enough to blister.

He unsnapped Randy's loose hobbles, threw the saddle over the big buckskin's back, lashed his roll tight. His movements were loose and easy. Two o'clock, he guessed. And it had to be a hundred and twenty in the shade. A bad time to be climbing over naked rock, but Seevers had disappeared beyond that first line of razorbacks. Blaine could only follow.

The buckskin, rested, climbed easily. Blaine let him pick his own way over the rock-strewn trail, finding his own pace. Blaine rode with his eyes three-quarters lidded against the glare off the rock. His body swayed in unconscious rhythm to the horse's gait. He might have been asleep, but he wasn't. He was aware that Seevers might have stopped running. He could be cunning enough to guess that Blaine would have figured out where he was going, would be hurrying and growing careless. These rocky hills, and the pass toward which Blaine was now heading, offered plenty of cover for an ambush.

Blaine's mind was empty as he rode, but it was receptive to any warning signals from his senses. Nothing else. In the past year he had learned not to think too much. Given rein, his mind could lurch in unexpected directions, dredging up horror when he wasn't ready for it.

A man used to the saddle, used to days and nights of riding toward distant goals, will often plumb his world and his own being deeper than a busier man, if he has any bent that way at all. It had never surprised Blaine to find a philosopher in every bunkhouse. In his loneliness the rider peopled his universe with thoughts. He opened himself to the sense of wonder and made the stars his friends.

There had been a time when Blaine had used his days and nights along cattle trails to make plans, to work things out, to dream. The dreams came first, the working out turned them into something more. A man with hours to mull over a question will find more answers than someone in haste.

But the dreams then had been good ones, not nightmares.

The plans had been for Samantha, or for the two of them together, and the children they would have.

He made no plans now; there were none to make, beyond finding the men he hunted.

And he had learned to ride empty, his mind like a room with its only door closed and locked, its windows boarded up, storm tight.

Now there was only the day's heat leaning against him like a solid weight, his narrowed eyes the only thing alive in his scorched face, bright as fish breaking the surface of a dark pool to flash briefly in the light. There was the steady clop of the buckskin's hoofs against rock, the long shadows hard in the slanting rays of the afternoon sun, the dust lingering in the air, as if someone has passed by here recently to stir it up.

But no one had. In these dry hills a puff of air could raise whatever dust there was. Blaine had already passed the safest hiding places, notches and shelves among the rocks overlooking the trail. Now he was certain that Lem Seevers, less than eight hours ahead of him, had not dared to risk his lead. He lacked the stamina, physical and moral, to lie so many hours in waiting.

Blaine did not know what Seevers looked like, but he was beginning to think he would recognize him if he saw him up close. The meager descriptions he had of a black-bearded man of average size would fit half the men he met on the plains, but he was beginning to know the man himself. The dartings of a mind that wasn't used to looking far ahead but reacted to whatever happened, finding one answer for today, another for tomorrow. The guilty sourness of stomach and heart that made him surly. The animal cunning that had tricked Blaine into following a false trail. The weakness that had made him follow Abe Stillwell's lead in momentary lust as it had in stealing or killing—the same weakness that made him dangerous as well as vulnerable. The callous cruelty that was killing the pinto to no purpose, for it was gaining him no ground. Blaine had little doubt that he would know Seevers when he ran him to ground. He would recognize the man's soul in his eyes.

It was late afternoon when the trail crested at last, after a much longer climb than Blaine had reckoned. Distances in this empty land were always deceptive. The height of a hill, or the space between two hills, was almost impossible to judge when measured only against the desert and the sky.

At the top of the pass Blaine paused in the giant shadow between the two great halves of a cleft rock—like an apple split—and looked across a broad, inviting valley far below. The drop on the southern flank of these razorbacks was much steeper than on the north side; he would reach the valley floor in half the time he had taken climbing. The valley seemed to be open-ended—at least the hills did not close in as far as he could see in either direction. Beyond it to the south, rising out of early purple shadows into golden sunlight, was another line of forbidding granite hills and towers. Seevers ought to be there by now, Blaine thought, into those shadowy sandstone breaks.

Unless he believed himself further ahead than he was. In that case he might have thought it safe to stop.

Blaine's gaze pulled back to find the cluster of buildings on the valley floor, small black specks that identified the headquarters of a ranch. Near them was the wriggling line of a creek that wormed its way along the east side of the valley. Its source was somewhere to the west, in these hills, and Blaine thought he caught a thread of silver in its bottom. Instinctively he appraised the ranch with a cattleman's eyes, critically approving. There was grass, brown at this time of year and patchy where it had been cropped or trampled. If that creek didn't tend to run dry, and if the valley were as open at the eastern end as it appeared . . .

He checked himself, almost tricked by old habit into thinking, remembering.

His mind closed.

He started the steep descent, watching as he went the plume of dust that writhed across the valley, fattening as it rose above the floor like a thick white worm. Not Seevers, he knew. There was more than one rider, and they were heading, as he was, toward the ranch.

# FOUR

They watched him ride in—a couple of waddies lounging beside a bunkhouse, curious in the idle way of men of their kind, and another group bunched around the long porch of the ranch house. These separated into the figures of three men and a woman as Blaine drew near. He noted three trail-dusty horses tied at a rail near a water trough and a stone well at one side of the yard.

There was also another man. This one showed no curiosity. He was wrapped in oilcloth—probably his own ground sheet, Blaine thought—and draped across the saddle of one of the horses. Red hair showed at one open end of the roll.

The fact that the dead man had not been cut loose, and

that all three horses at the rail still carried their saddles and packs, seemed to mean that the two riders Blaine had watched across the valley from the south didn't plan to stay long.

A tall man, hatless, his thick shock of hair completely white, strolled across the yard to greet him. He was a man in his fifties, with a long face deeply creased from nostrils to jaw line, the two seams framing his mouth and chin. He carried his left arm bent. It wasn't a withered arm, but it seemed shortened and unable to straighten, as if it had been improperly set at some time after being broken. The blue eyes that studied Blaine were mild.

"Howdy," Blaine said. He did not dismount.

"Evening," the tall man answered. "You come through the Cinders?" He nodded toward the razorbacks Blaine had crossed.

"If that's what they're called."

"They're called that. Likely because it can be hot as hell's own fire this time of year. You look as if you and your horse might be thirsty."

"I'd be obliged."

"Name's McAlister," the white-haired man said. Then, with a trace of pride, "This is my spread."

"I'm Blaine."

"Well, you're welcome to climb down and test your legs, Mr. Blaine. There's a spare bunk if you're not in a hurry, and no shortage of grub."

"I won't trouble you."

"No trouble, Mr. Blaine," McAlister said firmly. "Strangers are always welcome here."

"Maybe he is in a hurry." Another man had moved away

from the porch and across the yard. He was a thin, round-shouldered rooster in black twill, wearing hundred-dollar boots and a fine black Stetson. There was a gleam of pearl on the butt of his six-shooter and a badge pinned to the pocket of his shirt under the coat flap. He had very quick, sharp eyes and a drooping brown mustache that hid his mouth. There was an unexplained skepticism in those eyes, as if the expression were permanently there, and Blaine caught a hint of challenge in his tone. "That so, Blaine?"

Stepping down, Blaine walked Randy to the water trough. He'd given the horse a short drink in the trickle of the creek and walked in from there, so it was safe to let him drink what he wanted now. Unhurrying, Blaine turned to let his gaze rest on the lawman briefly, his face expressionless. He didn't like the kind of man who butted in on someone else's talk, but he didn't bristle over trifles. "No more than average," he murmured.

"This here's Marshal Holifield," McAlister said. "J. P. Holifield," he added in a tone that suggested the name should mean something to Blaine. It didn't, although there was something vaguely familiar about it. "Mr. Armstrong there is his deputy."

Blaine nodded briefly. Holifield was watching him closely, as if searching for a reaction. He surely was a sharp-eyed man, Blaine thought.

And he might have seen Lem Seevers.

"That your cargo?" Blaine asked, nodding toward the body in the oilcloth roll.

"It is," Holifield snapped. He volunteered nothing more.

"You might as well know," McAlister said soberly. "The marshal is hell on the hoof when it comes to trackin' down outlaws in these parts. Ain't the first time you've stopped at this trough, J.P., with the kind of cargo that don't carry a thirst."

Holifield grunted.

Blaine noticed that the woman had left the porch, disappearing into the house. It must be near suppertime, he thought, the reminder causing his belly to rumble. He peered off toward the granite hills to the south. "Might that be because Price's Landing is off there, Marshal?"

The lawman took a step closer, his interest clear. Blaine could see his mouth now under the screen of his mustache. It wasn't so much hidden as it was thin, lipless, as if he were biting down hard on something. "What do you know of Price's Landing, Blaine?"

"I been followin' a man might be making tracks that way. Maybe you seen him. Name of Seevers. Wears a black beard and rides a pinto with its markings covered."

"Maybe. Any special reason you're lookin' for him?"

The response told Blaine nothing. J. P. Holifield was not the kind of man who gave out information freely, he thought.

"Why, he come through here earlier on!" McAlister said. "Around noon, it was. You'll find that sorry pinto in the meadow behind the corral. Fellow who rode him didn't call himself Seevers, but his beard was black, like you say. He wanted a fresh horse and didn't much care if he took the worst of the bargain." McAlister turned toward Holifield. "I had no reason to question him, J.P."

Holifield shrugged off the explanation. "You haven't answered my question, Blaine," he said coldly.

Blaine looked at him. He didn't bristle over trifles, but

33

the lawman was crowding him. "I didn't hear you answer mine," he said easily.

The reply caused J. P. Holifield's narrowed eyes to darken. They locked with Blaine's for a silent moment. In that brief study the lawman seemed to see something in Blaine that he had not bothered to notice before, something as cold and unyielding as the hard core of his own being. He quickened to it, reacting as most men did, as if that toughness threatened him.

"You a bounty hunter?" he snapped.

"No."

"You have a reason for chasing a man to Price's Landing." This was a statement, not a question.

"I have." The brevity of the reply carried its unspoken message: the reason was personal.

There was another moment of hostile appraisal. Then the white-haired rancher intruded. "Turn your horse into that pasture, Mr. Blaine," he said. "You'll see your friend's pinto there. You'll stay for supper, surely? What about you, Marshal? Sure you won't reconsider and stop the night? Mrs. McAlister would take it as a pleasure to have you sit down to table with us."

"We'll be riding," Holifield said curtly. He glanced at his deputy Armstrong, a young fellow in his early twenties with an open, eager face. Armstrong reacted quickly, starting toward his horse. "We'll be halfway to town before the light's gone. This one needs to be buried soon, in this heat." The marshal's glance flicked indifferently over the dead man's roll. "I reckon Blaine's business will be taking him away as well."

"I reckon not," Blaine said, making the decision in that

moment. It had as much to do with the marshal trying to make up his mind for him as with the promise of a hot meal.

"Then you'll join us in the house. If the marshal prefers beans to beef, and a ground blanket to a bed, it doesn't mean every man has to." McAlister softened the words with a grin, but it was plain that his humor was uneasy where J. P. Holifield was concerned. The marshal would make many a man uneasy, Blaine thought.

He led Randy across the yard toward the corral as Holifield and his deputy released their horses from the rail. The deputy had the dead man's horse on a lead. Blaine heard their voices behind him as he swung past the corral toward the fenced pasture behind it, and then the quick steps of Holifield's horse catching up to him.

When Blaine stopped at a gate to strip down the buckskin, the marshal pulled up near by. "I'll see you again, Blaine," he said. "Any man who has business that takes him toward Price's Landing interests me. Maybe you and me will have business of our own."

"I doubt that."

Holifield's thin smile was cold. "Not for you to say. The law is my affair. You'll do well to remember it."

It's mine, too, Blaine thought. He was clear-eyed enough, even looking into himself, to see something mirrored in J. P. Holifield. The difference was he didn't wear a badge.

"Then you'll have no interest in me," he said.

He turned his back. He could feel the marshal's probing stare for another moment before he rode away.

The clatter of an iron triangle summoned Blaine and a trio

of cowpunchers from the bunkhouse, where he had dropped his gear. Supper was served at a long table in a big room added onto one end of the main house, next to the kitchen. The meal was made hearty by chunks of beef simmered tender and served in a thick stew with gravy and vegetables and potatoes, along with corn bread and coffee and pie. It was almost too much for Blaine's stomach to handle, strung tight as it was by leaner fare.

The meal was eaten mostly in silence. Blaine wasn't certain if it was made awkward by his presence or by the uneasiness of the crew in Iris McAlister's company. After a while he concluded the woman was the reason. The rough-hewn punchers, unruly among themselves, here ate with their eyes on their plates, their battered hands fumbling cautiously with white china and matched cutlery. When they sneaked a glance at the woman it was quick and furtive from under their brows; Blaine wondered if they ever saw any more of her than was visible from the waist down, what they could see with their heads lowered. They had names—Brazos Bill, Foster, Skinner—but they were typical of many of their breed, interchangeable with hired hands on any Kansas farm or cattle spread from Montana south to the border. Only one was a standout, Brazos Bill, and only because of his size. He was just too big for a cowpuncher, inches taller than Blaine and thicker everywhere, big arms and meaty thighs and a full belly going soft; you wondered what kind of a horse he could find to carry him. These were not fighting men, Blaine saw, but easygoing cowpokers who worked hard and asked little pay as long as it was regular. McAlister must not feel threatened.

Asahel McAlister had married late, at fifty taking a

young wife less than half his age. They were childless. The woman was as much of a surprise to Blaine as she must have been to the cattleman's crew. She seemed more like McAlister's daughter than his wife, and he seemed to treat her that way, with a father's pride rather than a husband's touchiness.

Iris McAlister had hair the color of the palest bleached grasses in this valley where she lived, eyes as clear and blue as the desert flowers that bloomed on the slopes in spring. Her lips were soft and ripe, full at the centers. She wore a long dress of blue and white checks, nipped in to a narrow waist that emphasized the womanly swell of hip and bosom. She seemed eager to please, anxious over having company to supper, and she was altogether too pretty to be believed. Cullom Blaine, a silent man anyway, found himself sharing the crew's constraint in her company. Like the others he avoided looking at her directly.

He felt no physical unease, although Iris McAlister was woman enough to stir any man's blood. That part of him was dead. It was memories he avoided; they were less easily buried.

The three hands—two others were at the far end of the range and would not be in for the night—ate quickly, mumbled thanks, scraped back their chairs and left. Blaine started to follow them but McAlister stopped him. "You can smoke in here, Mr. Blaine. Mrs. McAlister's permission."

Somewhat reluctantly Blaine relaxed in his chair, taking his time about rolling a cigarette. It turned out that the white-haired rancher felt obliged to explain J. P. Holifield.

"I'm surprised you haven't heard of our marshal," he

said. "Though I expect it's men on the dodge who have reason to know of him. And fear him."

"Like the one he had in tow?"

McAlister nodded. His wife sat with head bowed, as if she were not listening. "Name of Greiner, Holifield said. There's a price on his head. I reckon there is on most of the high-riders at Price's Landing."

"Seems like you're sittin' the hoop of a powder keg, this close to an outlaws' roost. How far is it?"

"Less than two days' ride. You could make it between sunup and sundown if it was all on the level, but those badlands are hard goin'. I reckon Sam Price figgered it that way. It's hard goin' in, and with the marshal waiting somewheres along the trail, it's lately been harder comin' out."

"You know Sam Price?"

"I met him once." McAlister hesitated. "He's treated me square."

"They don't bother you none?"

"No. I reckon they butcher a beef sometimes, but I'll not quarrel over that when it's done for eating."

Blaine nodded absently. Obviously McAlister's valley was vulnerable to a band of desperate men hidden somewhere in those hills to the southwest, but it must suit Sam Price's purpose to keep hands off, to have this buffer between himself and the more civilized world that called him outlaw. McAlister's place was a kind of way station where a man on the run, like Lem Seevers, could trade his tired horse for a fresh one, or take water and even rest if there were no hounds baying close at his heels. In a sense, then, the ranch was under Sam Price's protection because it was useful to him. The hunted thieves and fly-by-nights who sought out Price's sanctuary would know better than to harm McAlister—or his young wife.

But how predictable were such men? Blaine would not have put Iris McAlister in the way of such danger, no matter what assurances he had.

But he had done no better for his own, the thought snaked through; he had done worse.

He looked up to find the woman watching him, something alert and puzzled in blue eyes that had seemed only guileless before. He wondered in passing what she had seen in his face to awaken a woman's interest for the first time.

Blaine said, "Your marshal seems to take it personal, Price bein' where he is, holding out a welcome to wanted men."

"He does," McAlister agreed. "That's exactly the way he feels about it. Wasn't always that way, but it's like J.P. declared war sometime last spring. No one knows what started it, if there was anything. Some say he had a run-in with Price hisself. Others tell about some of that wild bunch raising hell in Tuckerville when the marshal was out of town, and I know that happened for a fact. Whatever, he means to clean out the whole bunch, one way or another, and makes no bones about it. Way I hear, he's let some ride in just so's they could carry the word that any man who tries to leave will find J. P. Holifield standin' across the trail."

Blaine considered this. If he rode into those hills after Seevers, Holifield would take it only one way, even if he found no reward dodger bearing Blaine's name or his likeness on it. He was the kind of man in whom an idea would be hard to uproot, once it took hold.

"Seems like he's takin' on a lot, your marshal."

McAlister looked at him keenly. "He don't look very big, Mr. Blaine, but he was cradled on cholla spines for sure."

"He's a hateful man!" Iris McAlister burst out unexpectedly. Both men looked at her in surprise.

"Now, Iris, honey, that's no way to talk about J.P." McAlister spoke in a father's cajoling tone of gentle remonstrance to a favorite. "The marshal does his duty, is all."

"He's the same as those others," she insisted, her chin lifting, defiant. "He wears a badge, that's all, or he'd be the same as Sam Price or any of them."

"That's not for you to judge, my dear—"

"It is when he brings his dead to my door!" she cried. "He likes killing, Mr. McAlister, you know that's true!"

She rose abruptly from the table and retreated to the kitchen, where a clattering of dishes continued to express her feelings. McAlister's eyes, following her, were tolerant, a little baffled. He's too old to understand her, Blaine thought, even the little a man can plumb a woman's nature.

"I'm afraid Mrs. McAlister has been upset this past fortnight. A youngster passed through she took a liking to. He was no more than a boy, and . . ." The rancher shrugged.

Blaine guessed the rest. The hurt in a woman who had lost her own youth without knowing how it had happened, maybe because she had had no other choice open to her, and the pain when she had seen the boy come back in a roll across his horse's back, on J. P. Holifield's lead.

Iris McAlister returned to the table carrying the enameled coffeepot. Her eyes were calm. "You'll have more coffee, Mr. Blaine?"

40

"Yes, ma'am. It's a long time since I've eaten so well," he added.

The white-haired rancher smiled, pride rising to his eyes as he regarded his wife. "No woman in West Texas sets a finer table," he said. "No, you can make that all of Texas!"

She smiled. "You haven't sampled so many, Mr. McAlister, that you can make such a boast."

"I've had fifty years of chewing beef tough enough to lay tracks with, and gravy you could use to grease wagon wheels, and biscuits better used to caulk holes in a wall," he answered good-humoredly. "That's experience enough."

Cullom Blaine felt a twist of envy, bitter as dregs. It had been a mistake to stop here, he thought. In the past year he had ridden by many a house on the plains in the quiet of evening, seeing warm light spill out to puddle the darkness, hearing voices and laughter. He had always known better than to stop. He had wanted information about Price's Landing from Asa McAlister, and he had let that need betray him.

"Is something wrong, Mr. Blaine?"

He looked into blue eyes, saw full lips parted. His own eyes were bleak, hardened against sympathy. The momentary lash of emotion had passed and he felt only the familiar emptiness, cellar-cold.

"No, ma'am. Except that I must take Mr. McAlister's side against you. You can't deny two men's samplings of Texas food." He scraped back his chair, rising, wanting to leave, the polite words falling from his lips like stones. "I can see why Mr. McAlister was so thankful to the Lord for His bounty."

41

"Hear, hear, well said!" Asa McAlister roared with delight. "What have you to say to that, hon'?"

Her cheeks coloring, the young woman did not reply. Her husband beamed at her, for all the world as if she had just won praise for her dancing, or for reciting a familiar passage well.

Blaine sat on the long porch, smoking, where McAlister had joined him after supper. Now the tall rancher had left to talk to Skinner, foreman of his crew. Blaine could hear their voices drifting across the dusty yard from the bunkhouse. It had been warm inside the house, the day's heat boxed in, but on the porch the air was cool and fresh. In the blue of evening the valley seemed peaceful, remote from any violence. It wasn't, Blaine thought. There was danger curling under every rock, and it could strike without any rattle of warning. He wondered if Iris McAlister knew that yet, if she had known it when she came.

He felt her presence without seeing or hearing her. The door had made no creak, and he turned his head quickly.

"No, don't get up, Mr. Blaine. It's nice and cool out here."

"Yes."

"The best time of day."

He nodded, silent.

"You'll be leaving us in the morning?"

"Yes."

"For Price's Landing?"

Blaine peered at her. She leaned one hip against the porch railing, wrapped an arm around a post. Light from the window behind them slanted across her bodice, leaving

42

her head and shoulders in shadow. "Yes."

"Why, Mr. Blaine?"

He wondered at the difference between men and women. None of the punchers in the bunkhouse would have asked that question, counting it his own affair. "What makes you ask?"

"You're different from the others. You're not on the dodge—I've seen too many of them pass this way. They always seem to be . . . looking over their shoulders. And you're not a drifter."

"You don't know anything about me, Mrs. McAlister."

"I know what I see."

Seeing is believing. One of the more foolish saws people liked to quote, Blaine thought.

From the darkness she studied him. One side of his face was caught by the light behind him. It was a closed face, hard, and there was something intimidating in it that she couldn't name. It was . . . pitiless. Yes, that was it. He was a man who would give no pity or quarter, and ask none. Yet he did not frighten her, as some others had, even those she had seen only from a distance. Or as J. P. Holifield did, even when he smiled.

There was something else in Blaine, buried deep, walled in. The perception brought a shiver, not for him but for herself. For this was a fate she had begun to fear for herself. Asa McAlister was gentle and kind, and she didn't know what would have happened to her after her father's death if he hadn't come along to offer her marriage, security, a home, a position in life. She tried to please him, to be what he wanted her to be, but what he wanted was not a wife or even a real woman. He wanted someone clever and pretty, not quarrelsome, to tend a little garden and set his table and keep him company. When he came to her bed he acted like one of the men from the bunkhouse, afraid to look at her. . . .

And so she tried to be what he wanted her to be, out of gratitude, and sometimes she had a frightening glimpse of herself being smothered in kindness and pretense, a pretty ornament on the outside, the real person boxed in, invisible, as lost as the man this Blaine had once been was lost.

She had to smile then, feeling foolish. Mr. McAlister would chide her for such thoughts, albeit gently, indulgently. Blaine was right. She didn't know anything about him at all.

"You don't think much of our marshal, Mr. Blaine," she said suddenly.

"I have no reason to think anything about him at all."

"You should, if you're going to Price's Landing."

"Maybe."

"That young man my husband spoke of . . . at supper?"

Blaine looked up, his face expressionless. Only the movement showed his interest.

"He was younger than I am, Mr. Blaine. A boy. A towheaded boy. Marshal Holifield didn't even know his name. He shot him dead, but he didn't even know his name!"

"Did you, Mrs. McAlister?"

She felt the heat rise to her neck and cheeks, and she was glad of the shadows that hid her face. She saw the boy grinning at her, his freckled cheeks smooth and beardless, his eyes dancing. He was the only one, it seemed, who had ever looked her in the eye. He had made her feel young and silly, just seeing him. "Yes," she whispered. "I knew it.

Edward Coleman. I could have told the marshal, but I didn't."

"Why not?"

"What did it matter when he was dead? As you will be, Mr. Blaine, if you're not careful of our marshal."

Blaine rose abruptly, startling her, confronting her with blunt impatience. "No one's safe, Mrs. McAlister. You'd best learn that now, and remember it. Where I'm going there are men who would chew J. P. Holifield up and spit out the pieces. Might be your young rider was one of 'em, and deserved to be shot or hanged. Age has nothing to do with it, nor looks. A young rattlesnake carries the same poison as an old one, and he's quicker in the sun."

She flinched. Instinctively she retreated a step, pushing away from the rail, not so much from the harsh words as from something cold and implacable in the man before her, suddenly revealed. "You can't know that . . ." She faltered.

"No more can you. And I'm no different from the others, Mrs. McAlister. You can believe that." He paused, and she could hear the quick intake of his breath. "Thank you for your hospitality, ma'am. Good night."

"Wait . . ."

He tramped down the steps and stalked away from her into the darkness, a solid shape, moving like a big rock rolling down the side of a hill, as if he would roll over anything in his way. She heard her husband's greeting as he came toward the house, a curt reply. Then Blaine's shape melted into other shadows, swallowed up.

I was right about him, she thought, the intuition only strengthened by his outburst. It wasn't a silly fancy after all.

# FIVE

Among some red sandstone piles that formed a break between two slopes, one slanting down toward the level grassland, the other climbing more steeply to the base of higher bluffs, Cullom Blaine paused to gaze back across the valley. The brown and golden grasses stirred, although the morning seemed to hold no breath of wind. Black specks crawled across the floor far to the northeast. Cattle grazing. The heat seemed to rise from the valley floor and to radiate from the pink rocks around him as well as from the sky, which was turning as white as an iron in the fire. Already his shirt was wet, pasted to his spine, and the seat of his jeans was slick against the saddle leather.

He could no longer make out the ranch buildings on the far side of the valley. For a long time they had seemed to float on a thin sheet of heat haze, or dust, like a mirage, but now even that vision was gone.

A restlessness caused his wide shoulders to move. They lifted, turned, swiveling his head, swinging his gaze toward the trail ahead. He rode on.

He studied the slope above him. It was sparsely covered with scattered yucca, mesquite, clusters of rock. While it offered little cover, there was plenty in the irregular cliffs towering above the rise. McAlister had said this trail was the only easy way through these sandstone and granite hills, the higher bluffs made inaccessible by deep canyons and raw flanks that offered no passage. There was supposed to be a western route, but it was said to be long and dry and difficult, leading through inhospitable desert wastes that skirted Comanche hunting grounds. Anyone trying to reach Price's Landing would be funneled along the trail Blaine followed. Somewhere ahead there would be lookouts posted, and, if Sam Price was as shrewd and careful as Blaine guessed, easily protected natural gates.

The outlaws might not worry about stray riders this far off. Unless Seevers had friends there, anxious to help, eager to cut down the man who followed him. Seevers would have had a story ready, like the one he had told Billy Archer. Would a stranger be given a chance to answer it?

And so he watched. Listened. Tried to think of nothing but the terrain ahead, the tracks he followed, the places a bushwhacker might choose to hide. Yielded to the rhythmic motion of the buckskin, as much a part of it as the jingle of his saddle rig. Accepted the day's brutal heat, the sun so scorching that, once when he took off his battered black hat to scrape a sleeve across his forehead, mopping up the sweat that dripped down into his eyes, his neck burned from the brief exposure. Welcomed that mind-dazing heat, because there was no use fighting it. Let time crawl by, unnoticed. And willed his mind to remain empty, a receptacle only for messages from his senses.

And for a time he succeeded. Time slid by. The sun passed its zenith, dropped lower. The trail turned west. Soon the sun would be in his eyes. He passed through one phalanx of pink hills and descended into a shallow bowl, crossed it and climbed again. Cut through a high-walled canyon and reached some barren flats. No grass here, no breeze to temper the sullen heat. Even the tumbleweeds sat still. It seemed as if he had been riding forever, not just this day's ride but the interminable days behind him, as if he had known no other life.

In late afternoon another granite ridge loomed ahead. Fronting it, on the line toward which the trail led, a sentinel tower rose, pale and wavering in the heat waves that rose from the rocky table. McAlister had mentioned the landmark. When Blaine came to it he would be at the foot of the last and most severe climb. He was more than halfway to the Landing.

He plodded toward it, bleak-eyed, doing all the things he had schooled himself in for the last eleven months. In the end he failed. The oblivion of mind he sought was denied him.

The woman was the reason. Not only the firm, full breasts thrusting against the cotton of her bodice, straining the fabric. Not only the lean length of a thigh pressed against the bar of the porch railing, the wood digging into firm flesh. Not only the smell of her hair, strong as it was when he stood close to her there on the porch in the clear air of evening. Not any one of these things, female things, but all of them together, the fact of her as a woman, anxious and eager, timid and hopeful, passionate and alive. *Alive.*

That one evening in Iris McAlister's presence, even the final morning glimpse of her standing on the porch and shading her eyes as she stared after him when he rode away—as Samantha had always stood and watched until he was long out of sight, shading her eyes against the morning sun in the same gesture—had undone all of his bitter discipline, bringing everything back, astonishingly vivid, denying all these months of emptiness during which he had tried to seal the terrible memories along with the good ones in a box as closed and final as a coffin.

How easily it had happened again! Always he had to be on his guard against the chance meeting, the stray glance, the face at a window.

Samantha had not been as pretty as Iris McAlister. She had not been so young, so unmarked. Some might even have called her plain, though not Cullom Blaine. Her features were even enough, the nose and cheeks and mouth and eyes all in the right places. But the nose was high-bridged, a trifle sharp. The mouth was wide, the teeth prominent—she showed a real mouthful of teeth when she laughed. Her eyes were the only thing saucy about her—brown, weren't they? My God, how could he forget?—but their sparkle came from humor and intelligence, not silly vanity or invitation, as in some women. She had good shoulders, soft breasts, a narrow waist. But she herself believed that her hips were too broad, her thighs somewhat heavy, consoling herself that her shape should make child-bearing easier. Which hadn't been true. Blaine liked everything about her, but she was most proud of her hair. It was thick and heavy and dark, the color of rich chocolate. When she let it all the way down, at night when they were alone, it reached all the way to the hollow of her spine. He used to think, watching her hair spill down her back, released, that he was the only man who had ever seen it that way, and the thought always brought pleasure. She'd always known what he was thinking then, and he could see the smile begin deep in her eyes, and flow outward.

Most men who looked at her seemed to feel like smiling, rather than gulping or averting their eyes, the way they did with Iris McAlister. Nothing against that young woman. It was just that Samantha was different. She hadn't brought an instant color rising to a man's neck, a thickening of blood in his veins, a heat stirring in his loins, the way some women affected a man on sight.

She wouldn't have given them any provocation, the men who came that night. She hadn't invited them in. They had had to come looking for her. That was one of the things Blaine could never forget.

Not that there was any lack in her. Samantha was woman enough to keep a man anxious all of his life. She simply didn't parade what she was underneath those layers of calico and petticoats. She didn't sidle up to a man and look at him sidelong to tease him and to puff him up, like a dance hall chippy. More often she would say something to make him laugh or put him at his ease. Or to take him down a peg, if that was what he needed.

Even in that she made a man see the humor instead of causing him to feel belittled.

She had never lost that easy humor, even though Blaine had never made it easy for her. He had left her alone for weeks on end during the summer of their first year on the land he had bought, west of Martinsville. Most of the time he was back in the brush beating out a tiny herd of long-horns, all bone and gristle and horns. The shack they lived in that first winter wasn't fit for chickens, much less a woman used to a decent family house in Hardin, in the cotton country over east of the Trinity. There was no pro-tection on the north window during the heavy rains that came before winter really howled in. There was a mud floor and a roof that rained spiders and scorpions when it didn't turn into a waterfall. There wasn't even a door you could fairly give so fine a name to, just some hides nailed over the opening, until so much snow and sleet blew through the flap that Blaine was forced to patch a door together out of scraps and hang it.

That was winter. Spring proved no cause for celebration. At first they thought it was, during that early false green-up that teases grass and mules and men out of their holes. Blaine and Samantha celebrated, and then the weather turned bitter cold again. A wet spring followed, good for grass to fatten up those slab-sided longhorns but never easy, not for a woman left alone much of the time, in a leaky shack on a wild frontier.

It was never easy, and there were times when Samantha let Blaine know it. By nature she was a smiling woman, patient and tolerant of a man's faults and stumblings, but not always. She could spit fire and use her tongue like a whip to skin a man alive when she was angry—which wasn't often, and was generally earned. Blaine would rather have walked into the teeth of one of those Texas northers, or ridden bareback through a prairie fire, than face Samantha when she was in one of her rare moods of rage at him and fate and Texas.

But a man would always have come back to Samantha Blaine, as he did, remembering the smile after the storm died, like sunlight dazzling through black clouds.

The first herd Blaine drove north to Kansas had the fever. Everything imaginable happened to thin out the second, two years later, everything from swollen rivers to Indians demanding bounty to Kansas guns at the border. Samantha swallowed those disappointments without complaint, acting like she still believed that Blaine was right and not simply crazy to put his faith in the future of raising cattle in a land God had overlooked or consigned to madmen and rattlesnakes.

Blaine's third herd got through and paid a small return, but it was the fourth, which he had combined with two neighbors' beeves on a big drive, that justified all the hard years, the bitter isolation of the winters and the punishing work and hardship of the hot summers. That time Blaine came home with money and time and a feeling of pride that he would never know again, that pride that came from doing something for the first time that wasn't supposed to be possible, beating all the odds.

He started to build the house that summer. It was going to be a Texas house that would lock out snakes and snow and loneliness, a real house with glass in the windows and a piano in the parlor. Oh, he had long ago put planks down over the mud floor of the original shack, a wooden floor and a door that latched and a real fireplace that drew well and was big enough for cooking. But the new house was going to be what Samantha wanted, what Blaine had promised her in his heart.

Her and the boy. He kept thinking it was a boy.

Samantha had lost their first two, in difficult births that belied her sturdy woman's shape. Blaine had done a lot of cursing when they buried each, and Samantha had done an equal amount of praying to balance the scales. Now she was carrying again.

She was in her fourth month, and the new house was half finished. They had moved into the half that contained the cookhouse and dining hall, with a loft tucked up under the roof for sleeping until the other half of the house was built.

Blaine had put up the shell of that section, which would be their living and sleeping quarters when it was completed, and he had laid a roof of cedar shakes over the whole, the two cabins thus joined by a common roof with a covered dogtrot between them, open to the prevailing summer breezes.

In mid-September, her fourth month carrying, Samantha became ill. She made light of it, but her fever scared Blaine. He rode in to Martinsville to bring the doctor, his friend Tom Wills, out to the ranch to see her. He left at sunup, intending to be back before dark, but Wills was away on another errand of mercy. He did not return to town until it was long after dark. Wills was stumbling weary, and Blaine, remembering Samantha's assurances that she would be fine, did not press him into another long ride without rest.

Blaine slept that night at the hotel, but only for the few hours he thought Tom Wills needed. He roused the doctor while it was still dark and they set off, hoping to reach the ranch in good time for the hearty breakfast Blaine promised.

They saw the smoke from a long way off. Wills made a comment, pointing, and Blaine frowned uneasily. A prairie fire was never a minor worry. But he didn't feel real concern until they were closer and he could see how swiftly the black column was climbing, and that it was not racing like a grass fire but localized. And whatever was burning was not only close to home but right *there*, right where he had chosen his spot and built his house, a stone's throw from Walnut Creek where it spilled between two low, rounded hills.

He kneed his horse into a run. Fear was at his back. Something cold pressed against the back of his skull where it joined his neck. A strange kind of wildness took hold of him.

The last few miles seemed to take forever. Blaine broke past a stand of cedar, where he had cut wood for the first shack and all of the splits for the roof of the new saddlebag house. He reached the creek and swept around a rise, and the awful, unimaginable scene burst upon him.

The house was engulfed in flames and smoke. A great black pillar climbed straight up. He could see the live red flames and hear a continuous crackling like gunfire. He was shouting then, although he didn't know it, screaming her name: "Samantha! My God, Sam! Sam!" He didn't know where Tom Wills was, if he had kept up or fallen behind. He was leaning over the buckskin's neck, his spurs raking the horse's sides, the blood pounding in his temples.

He couldn't see her. Where was she? God in heaven, she couldn't be inside, she would have been able to get out. Why couldn't he see her?

He hit the bottom of the knoll and reined in hard. Spilled out of the saddle, running too fast. Stumbled and sprawled onto his chest. He scrambled up. The heat of the flames seared his face and hands. The sound of them was a roar that filled his ears, blotting out everything else. He looked around wildly as he ran toward the house, knowing and not believing, refusing to believe that she could be trapped inside that hell's inferno.

The whole house was ablaze. The shell of the new section was already gutted. Part of the roof caved in with a sudden crash, collapsing into the unfinished shell.

He heard her scream.

In that instant Cullom Blaine saw something that froze his blood, stopped his heart, wiped all reason from his brain. The door had been boarded up—from the outside! The door and the window facing him. New boards had been nailed over the openings, wood taken from the pile Blaine had had ready for the interior of the living quarters, wood for bunks and tables and shelves.

He ran toward the door, shouting. The ceaseless roar of the flames drowned out his cries. That thunder overpowered all other sound. He couldn't even be sure if those were screams he heard from inside the burning house or if he imagined them.

But he knew. Knew because of the boards nailed over the door and windows. He tore at the boards with his bare hands. The heat blistered his flesh, seared his eyes, blinding him. The boards had been put up hastily, crudely. One pulled loose at one end. He ripped it aside, grabbed another.

Tom Wills was there. Blaine didn't know where he had come from. He was shouting into Blaine's ear, hauling at him with both hands. Trying to drag him away. Blaine couldn't hear Tom's words. He shrugged the doctor off and attacked the boards over the doorway.

She screamed. She was alive. No one could live inside that fire, but *she was alive.*

Wills threw himself onto Blaine's back. He was trying to stop him. Raging, Blaine threw his friend twenty feet across the yard with a strength he didn't know he had.

Another board split, a nail screeching. Blaine threw the piece away and tore the remainder off. The rest came easier. They hadn't needed to make a good job of it—even in that moment, raging, mindless, Blaine knew that someone had had to do this, that someone mad or unimaginably cruel had covered the openings. There could be only one reason for that cover, the need to pen someone or something inside that had to be destroyed.

The last boards offered hardly any resistance. He didn't bother with the two across the bottom. He lifted his leg and rammed a boot heel against the door. Weakened by the flames, it exploded inward. A solid blast of heat struck Blaine, driving him back against his will like a physical blow.

He was still half blind and he couldn't breathe. The heat scorched his flesh and burned his clothes and knifed deep into his lungs. He got up from his knees and tried to walk into that wall of fire, and it stopped him where reason could not.

Then something black and shapeless flew out through the open doorway, hurtling past him. It was Samantha, and her long hair was a living torch.

Blaine stumbled toward her. He fell and couldn't get up. He had to crawl the last few feet. *Samantha!* He threw himself on top of her, trying to smother the flames with his own body. He rolled her and himself in the dirt of the yard. His blackened and blistered hands beat at the flames. Tears, unknown and unheeded, made rivulets in the blackness of his face.

Tom Wills appeared again. He too was black with smoke and ashes. He got his hands under Samantha's arms, under the raw flesh, for she was naked, and dragged her farther from the terrible heat of the burning house.

Blaine crawled after them.

They both heard it—a tiny bleat of sound. It struck to the very marrow of Cullom Blaine's being. He didn't want her to be alive now. His own pain from his burns was unbearable. He couldn't conceive of the pain she had endured. He didn't want her to suffer any longer.

But, unbelievably, she was still alive, clinging to one last spark, like a tiny ember still glowing in a dead fire. Her mouth was not a mouth any more, only a hole surrounded by a black crust, but it moved. And Blaine, placing his ear close to her featureless face, the face he had loved, heard another sound. "Still . . ." He waited. Her mouth moved again. "Still . . ."

She seemed to fall in on herself, like ashes collapsing, and was gone.

He could not have sworn to what she tried to say before the law, but he did in his heart. And for him Samantha's last utterance was more than an attempt to speak a name. It was also a request, a plea.

Tom Wills reported Samantha's death to the sheriff in Martinsville, Luke Shields. For a fortnight Blaine was on his back, recovering from severe burns. He came out of the fire with surprisingly little disfiguration. There were permanent scars on his hands and one leg, and there was a red patch high on his forehead that didn't show much, since it was generally half covered by his hat. Without knowing it at the time he had covered most of his face with his bandanna, and by lucky chance the neckerchief had not caught fire. His eyelids and lashes had been burned away, but the flesh was whole and they grew back in time.

While he was on his back the Clancy brothers and Wes

Hannifin, members of a well-known gang of trouble-makers and cow-lifters, were caught foolishly selling Lightning-B beef—Cullom Blaine's brand. All three men were carrying more money in their war bags than they could explain, and they were brought back to Martinsville for trial. Several others of the bunch escaped, including one known as their real leader, Abe Stillwell.

Stillwell. Still. Blaine needed no other proof. That was the name Samantha had tried to tell him.

He wasn't allowed to see the brothers or Hannifin, much less get close to them. At their trial, Blaine, not having been allowed into the courtroom with a gun, tried to get at Art Clancy, who was nearest him, with his bare hands. A half dozen men brought him down before he could reach Clancy. The judge took Blaine's testimony, but he wasn't allowed into the courtroom after that.

There was no real evidence linking Tom and Art Clancy, Wes Hannifin, and the rest of the Stillwell-Clancy gang to the burning of Blaine's house and Samantha's murder. Everyone knew they'd done it, but the judge admonished the jury that they had to decide on the evidence in the crime with which the outlaws were charged, and that alone. Tom Wills hadn't heard what Samantha said, and the judge seemed skeptical that Blaine could have heard anything intelligible under the circumstances.

The outcome was that the Clancy brothers and Hannifin were found guilty of cattle rustling, not murder. They escaped the rope and were sentenced to terms in the Texas Penitentiary at Huntsville, where Blaine could not get at them.

In time, when he was able to think more clearly, Blaine

pieced together the insane pattern of what must have happened, although the convicted thieves had denied any larger guilt to the last.

There had been a lot of talk in the territory about Blaine's successful spring drive. His herd had been twice the size of the two bunches thrown in with them, and the whole lot had fetched a high price in Kansas. And it was said that, because the bank in Martinsville had been robbed twice in little over a year, Blaine had placed no money there. It was supposed that he had it stashed away on his ranch, the way men will who don't trust banks.

Some men just talked too much, and there was no way of determining who had started the rumors about Blaine's money. Someone who had been on the drive, surely, but that could have been any of a score of ranchers and cowpokers.

It hadn't taken long for the word to reach one of the Clancy brothers or Abe Stillwell. Blaine had been back only two months at the time of the fire.

The irony was that the rumors were largely wrong. Blaine had invested a chunk of the money in another section of land adjoining his, a transaction not yet publicized. He had then deposited most of the rest in the bank at Meridian, placing little faith, as the stories rightly guessed, in the easily opened box at Martinsville. He came home, after paying off his crew, with less than twelve hundred dollars in cash, and he had made purchases out of that.

Blaine guessed that the raiders had found no more than nine hundred dollars in the cache in the cookhouse loft. Not so much to divide among a half dozen men or more.

Not much to risk a rope for, or to kill a woman for.

Tom and Art Clancy. Abe Stillwell. Wes Hannifin. Four certain names. To them Blaine added Brownie Hayes and Lem Seevers, two men who were seen with Art Clancy shortly after the fire. Another long rider named Tinker Wright was known to run with the gang. He would hardly have missed such easy pickings. There was a chance that one or two others might have been along. Blaine would learn their names in time.

Almost a year had passed since Blaine buried Samantha within sight of their original shack and the burned-out remains of the Texas house. Her grave was in shade, on a rise overlooking the creek. It had been more than ten months since he had been well enough to ride away, beginning his long search. In all that time he had tracked down only one man, Abe Stillwell. Blaine had run him down in Fort Smith in the spring. He had called him there.

Stillwell had laughed at him. He was a big, brawling man who was said never to have lost a fight, with fists or knife or six gun. He had been half drunk and unafraid of the haggard, dusty cowman who faced him in the street, a man inarticulate and quivering in his rage. Stillwell had bragged openly of what he'd done, taunting Blaine with it. That was how Blaine learned the rest of the story.

One of the gang had seen Blaine hanging around Martinsville all afternoon waiting for Tom Wills. When night came and it looked like Blaine would stay in town, he had carried word to the others. They had been planning the raid, waiting for the right time. If it hadn't been that night it would have been another, Stillwell assured Blaine, and he would have died along with his woman. But the way it worked out, it was easier than they could ever have planned it. They had come to the ranch around midnight, knowing that Blaine had let his summer riders go, not being able to keep a winter crew as yet, knowing that his woman was alone and he would not return before morning. That gave them all night to find the money.

Remembering the money made Stillwell angry. He remained convinced that Blaine must have had the rest buried somewhere, but his woman hadn't talked. They had found the cache in the loft without her telling them it was there.

But their search went on for the rest of it, and all the while a lusty woman was there for the taking.

They had put one man out as a lookout, taking turns at the chore. In the house they had tied the woman down, and they had taken turns with her as well. Oh, she'd screamed and hollered at first, Stillwell said, but after a while she had got to like it, and she begged them to come at her in ones and twos.

That was as far as Stillwell got with his story. Blaine drew on him. He ran straight at the gunman as he dragged out his Colt. Stillwell, as good as his reputation, started late and still beat Blaine by a half second. He shot for Blaine's heart.

Blaine's lurching run threw the outlaw's aim off by a couple of inches, no more, but the bullet stopped him in his tracks. That fooled Stillwell, and he made his one mistake. He neglected to squeeze off a second shot to make sure of his victim.

The bullet missed bone. It tore through the flesh of Blaine's left arm, the inner bicep, was deflected and creased his side. The impact stopped him, and blood showed on his vest. Abe Stillwell was waiting for him to fall when Blaine started shooting. His first ball struck the gunman full in the chest. The second tore off half his jaw. The third one missed, but Stillwell was already as good as dead.

Blaine had no regret over shooting a man who was half drunk, who would almost certainly have killed him if he'd been sober. Stillwell had been clearheaded enough to know who Blaine was and why he was dying. That was all Blaine cared about.

Abe Stillwell had fired the first shot. The rest was self-defense, and there were a dozen witnesses close enough to the shooting to clear Blaine of any charges.

The story of the fire and Cullom Blaine's long quest didn't reach the saloons in Fort Smith until a couple of days later. By then Blaine was gone.

He carried with him the names Stillwell had confirmed during his drunken boasting. One of them was Lem Seevers.

Blaine made a cold camp while it was still light. There were canyons ahead, and pitfalls he didn't want to stumble into in the dark.

And he wanted Sam Price's lookouts to see him coming.

He camped near the base of the rock tower, but he took the precaution of seeking out a ledge some twenty feet above the trail and off to the right, protected by a natural brow. He loose-hobbled the buckskin some thirty yards away in one of the myriad cuts that fanned away from the granite hills.

Not that a force of badmen couldn't have smoked him out.

But one man wouldn't be able to sneak up on him unseen.

Blaine felt exhausted, drained. The hard ride and the punishing heat weren't the reasons. He was emotionally wrung out. Remembering had done that. After nearly a year it was still the same.

Lying on the tiny ledge in bottom darkness as the night air cooled and a wind blew through holes in the stone tower, playing eerie notes as if it were a giant's flute, Cullom Blaine thought of J. P. Holifield. That reminded him of a friendlier lawman, Luke Shields, and what he'd said. "Let it go, Blaine. I know how you feel. Christ, any man would feel the same. But you can't buck them all alone even if you could find them. You'll only get yourself killed, and that won't bring Mrs. Blaine back. Men like that, they'll keep getting into trouble. They'll make mistakes, and sooner or later the law or their own miseries will bring them to account."

Tom Wills had said much the same, choosing almost the same words. Blaine had looked at him and said, "You were there, Tom. You saw her." And he had added, unnecessarily, "You know it wasn't only her. There was the boy as well, who would have been our son. You askin' me to forget that, Tom? Are you tellin' me I *can* forget it?"

Tom Wills had been silent, unable to answer him.

Seven months to track down Stillwell, Blaine thought. Nearly four more months to come within a day's ride of the second man, Seevers. It seemed like more, like half a lifetime.

That was why he couldn't turn back. He didn't know what lay ahead for him at Price's Landing, but he couldn't turn back now.

He listened to the wind playing in the rocks high above him, and at last, exhausted, he slept.

# SIX

From sunup the following day, which found him already two miles from his night camp, picking his way through rugged foothills toward a high range, Cullom Blaine knew that he was being watched.

Sam Price had picked his hideout well. A man could lose himself in a hundred blind ravines or along animal tracks that went nowhere, but only one trail led to Price's Landing. It was clearly marked and easy to follow. Sam Price obviously had no fear of a frontal assault. The trail climbed steadily now, and by mid-morning it brought Blaine to a steep, high-walled canyon. This giant fissure had been cut over untold centuries by what was now a narrow stream. In flood, Blaine thought, the bottom of the canyon would be under high water. Now it was dry except for the trickling stream, shallow and clear as it tumbled down over a bed of rocks. The narrow trail ran parallel to the water, in places no more than two feet of smoothed-down rock at the lip of the stream.

Blaine rode slowly. There had been a lookout, he guessed, at the top of one of the high ridges above the mouth of the canyon. From there a man would be able to scout the approaches from the north all the way to the next barrier of hills. From the dry flats past that sentinel tower and after, there was no way to approach secretively at all. In places there was sparse brush and scrub oak, stirrup high, but no cover adequate to hide a rider from keen eyes watching from the heights.

And there would certainly be others higher up the canyon who would pick up and relay a warning signal from the forward lookout point, or spot an intruder if the first sentry should have happened to fall asleep in the sun.

Blaine had seen no one, heard nothing, but he could feel the eyes boring into him all the way.

Halfway up the canyon the stream disappeared abruptly into a split in the rock wall on the left side of the trail. Somewhere in the heart of the mountain of rock was the underground spring that was the source of the water.

And this was Sam Price's water supply, Blaine saw. The trail widened out above the water, and there were parallel tracks cut deep into the rock floor. They were wagon tracks, made by wagons weighed down under heavy water barrels.

Blaine knew he was close.

He felt strong emotion—not exhilaration or excitement, but a lifting of his spirits, a feeling of relief that this long hunt was almost over.

It was up to Sam Price now. If the outlaw chief and his band of renegades sided with Lem Seevers, counting him one of their own, Blaine's search would end here in his own death.

He had bet his life on a wild card: the honor of thieves.

Slowly he eased Randy forward. The clop of the buckskin's hoofs was sharp and clear within the high-walled canyon. Then, less than a half mile above the source of the creek, these walls began to break up into huge, grotesque formations of pink rock, sculpted by wind and weather into the shapes of spires and domes and saddle peaks worn smooth. The trail remained in deep shadow, but the pink rock ahead and above Blaine caught fire in the sunlight. Under his shirt Blaine's body ran with sweat.

Clearly audible from up-canyon came the slide of a rifle bolt, the click of a hammer. "That's far enough!" a harsh voice commanded. "Both hands on the horn, stranger, and keep 'em there. That's jest fine. Now you can ease up closer. Make a sudden move and it'll buy you wings."

Blaine rode past a big shoulder into bright sunlight at the top of the trail.

Three men faced him there. All three held rifles aimed at his chest. Two of the men were at ground level, while the third sentry watched him from a perch above the trail that offered a long view down the canyon. All three beard-stubbled faces were hostile, slit-eyed with suspicion.

"Your name Blaine?" The speaker had a big square jaw that looked hard enough to break a fist on. On the other hand the shapeless nose above it had been broken too many times.

"Yes."

"He's the one," Square Jaw said to the others. "You must be some kind of a fool, Blaine."

"Maybe."

"No maybe about it. Get his iron, Chico. We'll watch him."

A squat, bowlegged man with a dark Indian face trotted forward. Blaine made no move as Chico jerked his Colt from its holster and his rifle from its scabbard. Square Jaw waited until Chico had stepped back before he spoke again, addressing the third man.

"Harley, you ride on ahead and tell Sam I'm bringin' him

in. You won't have need of those lead-throwers no more, Blaine. We don't welcome bounty hunters here with anythin' but a rope. You've bought your last drink with the price on another man's head!"

# SEVEN

Sam Price was a burly man, clean-shaven, with a mass of curly black hair that was almost shoulder-length. More black hairs sprouted from his nostrils and ears, from the open neck of a leather shirt, and from the cuffs of his sleeves. When he took a bath, Blaine thought, he must look like a bear.

Price also had a distinctively drooping left eyelid, created by an old knife wound. Someone had tried to scoop out the eye and missed, though he had left his mark. Blaine wondered if Price favored a knife in a fight. If so, it was hidden up one of his sleeves or in a boot sheath. The six-shooter at his hip was in plain sight. His eyes were small and deep-set, black as ebony, and his smooth cheeks were almost as swarthy as Chico's, dark enough to suggest some Mexican or Apache blood.

Prodded at gun point into the bandit leader's presence, Blaine returned his cold gaze in silence but with thoughtful appraisal. To give his name to a hideout for a small army of gunslingers and assorted Daniel Boones, to hold sway over the cat-eyed badmen Blaine had observed on his way into the camp, Sam Price had to be a tougher *cabrón* than any of them. There was little doubt that he would have had to win his place in a score of fights, like the lead stallion of any wild bunch, before his reputation had become formidable enough to cause newcomers to accept his right to set down rules and enforce them without a battle. Even now he must occasionally face a challenge from some short-trigger man who couldn't accept second place to anyone.

Blaine's first full view of Price's Landing had startled him. The camp was situated on a level table sheltered by an immense, curving wall of rock, reaching some fifty feet above the table and hollowed out into an enormous cave. Against the back wall of the cave was a warren of eroded smaller caves and crumbling stone shelters piled one on top of the other, climbing the wall in a series of shallow ridges. Old Indian caves, Blaine realized, studying them in surprise. He had seen their like before in New Mexico. Crude ladders or stone steps led from one level to another, and there was activity here and there, confirming that some of the men of the Landing found those ancient shelters adequate living quarters.

At ground level a half-dozen low, adobe buildings sprawled across the opening of the main cave, which was more than two hundred feet wide. These buildings were fashioned entirely of mud bricks except for the ceiling poles, whose ends projected beyond the walls. Those roof poles would have had to be hauled up the canyon, for there were no trees in these rocky heights. Smoke came from the chimney of one long building, and the presence of water barrels and a garbage pit told Blaine that this was the main cookhouse for the camp, which was really a small village. Sounds of raucous laughter and argument from another building suggested that it might be the camp's saloon. Three long, narrow buildings of identical size and shape were probably barracks where most of the men of the camp slept. There was also one small, windowless hut with a single narrow plank door carrying a big padlock, and, finally, the large building to which Blaine had been escorted. It seemed to be a kind of meeting place, or head-quarters. It was one long room. At one end was a table facing the entrance. Sam Price sat behind it, alone. Flanking it on either side were two other long tables with benches. Three men sat at each of these tables, indolently smoking and eying the stranger who had been seated on a backless stool facing Sam Price. The square-jawed sentry who had brought Blaine in remained standing behind him at the council hall door, holding his rifle ready.

Sam Price had things well organized, Blaine thought. If he had guessed right, Price would also have a set of rules that the men who came under his sway would have to accept and obey.

"Shaughnessy says you admit to being called Blaine," Price said after his prolonged study of the prisoner.

"That's right."

"You don't deny it."

"I have no reason to."

"Then you must find this world a tiresome place to live in. You know who I am?"

"You'll be Sam Price, I reckon."

"And this is Price's Landing. This is my town, and I run it," Price declared, giving the camp a more dignified name than it seemed to deserve. "But we've also got our town council, and that council has a say in everything that's done here. That includes deciding whether any man who comes is allowed to stay or leave, and it includes listenin' to any complaint against any man. You savvy so far, Blaine?"

"Seems clear enough."

"You don't sound like you're worried much."

"Should I be?"

"You're damned right you should be! You got plenty reason to worry. Most every man here has a price on his head, I reckon you know that. The word on you says you're a bounty hunter."

"That's a lie." Blaine glanced around the hall. The six councilmen were all watching him. There wasn't a friendly eye among them. Would these be the men to vote on whether he was allowed into the camp? Or allowed to live?

"What made you come here if you wasn't lookin' to profit? You don't have the smell of no holdup man, Blaine."

"I'm not."

Sam Price leaned forward. His good eye seemed to leer at Blaine. "What makes you think you'd find a welcome here? We don't hold no church meetings, Blaine. Or did you maybe steal a horse or slit your woman's throat?"

Cullom Blaine stifled his anger, but he could not keep the bitter hatred from his voice. "None of those. I came here because I'm following a man who raped a good woman and boarded her inside her house and set fire to it while she was still alive! His name is Seevers, and I know he's here because I was less than a day behind him and this is where his tracks brought him. I rode in after him, because I thought you'd welcome any honest-to-God holdup man or high-line rider, but I figgered maybe you might not bed down so easy with the kind of man this Seevers is, the kind of cold-foot skunk that would take a woman who was carrying her child and use her like he did, and ride off laughing while she started to beg and scream." He paused when his voice began to shake. "Seevers is all I want. All I'm askin' you for is the chance to face him."

Price sat back in his chair, frowning now. His glance flicked briefly left and right, and Blaine knew without looking that the men of the council were more attentive now. He could feel the subtle change in the atmosphere of the hall, the dropping away of indolence, the consideration of something that had seemed cut-and-dried a moment before.

"There's no one name of Seevers in the Landing," Price said.

"I don't give a damn what he calls himself. He wears a black beard and he would've got here some time yesterday or last night. He's ridin' a horse he traded from Asa McAlister two days ago. It should show McAlister's brand."

There was no reaction in Sam Price's black eyes, no indication that Blaine's words had confirmed what he knew. After a moment the outlaw leader said, "If such a man came here, when he did he put himself under the protection of Sam Price and every man in this camp. That's our rule, and if we was to break it, then it wouldn't be worth no more than a painted cat's smile. Why should we break it for you?"

"Are you saying you protect the murderers of women and children?"

There was a muttering from one of the side benches. Sam Price looked angrily at the source of the interruption, as did Blaine. Two men were exchanging words, a third was scowling at Blaine. He couldn't read the scowl.

One of the two men who had been arguing spoke up. He

71

had the long-faced, mournful look of a cowman who had just lost his last calf, but the gray eyes brooding over deep pouches were thoughtful. "This woman you're talkin' about," he said. "She be your wife?"

"That's right."

"I'll ask the questions," Price snapped.

"It's the council has to vote," the other retorted.

"By God, it's me named you to this council, Taggart!"

"Hold on now, Sam. Goddamnit, it was agreed the council was supposed to decide these things, not any one man, not even you."

"The council advises. Sam Price decides!"

Taggart—the long-faced man in the middle on the bench to Blaine's right—was angry enough not to give it up. "Hell you say! That ain't the way it's supposed to be." He looked around for support. Blaine guessed that several others might be on his side, but they were reluctant to say so out loud if it meant Sam Price's ire.

"You tellin' me how to run my own council?" Price's tone turned soft. There was something baleful in his hooded stare, a clear warning in the lowering of his voice.

"Hell, it ain't just *your* council, Sam," Taggart complained, but his tone was now more aggrieved than insistent. He was backing off. "I mean, it's supposed to be for all of us."

Price stared at him for a long moment, facing him down, forcing Taggart and the others to see that he had been compelled to back away from a direct confrontation. Then, seemingly satisfied, Price said, "You'll get your chance when I'm done, and when we vote. You got anythin' else to say, you say it then." He turned to Blaine. "How do we know you ain't lyin'?"

"How do you know Seevers isn't? You can prove it out if you want. My name's Cullom Blaine. I have a spread over near Martinsville. Seevers was runnin' with Abe Stillwell a year ago over that way, him and some others. They raided my place one night when Mrs. Blaine was there alone. . . ." Blaine stopped. In spite of himself he was sweating. Telling the story aloud, parading it before men like these, was a hell of its own. And he'd entered it willingly, as most men rode into any kind of hell. After a moment he said, his tone flat now, devoid of emotion, "I tracked Stillwell down in Fort Smith last spring."

Sam Price cocked his head, his alertness revealing new interest. "You the one gunned Abe Stillwell down?" He sounded surprised.

"Yes. For the same reason I chased Seevers into this hole."

"I'll be damned."

Sam Price exchanged glances with the members of his council. All were now regarding Blaine with open curiosity. Abe Stillwell's reputation with a gun was widely known among them. The man who had killed him was an object of interest. He had gained some ground, Blaine knew. Five minutes ago all seven, Price included, had been ready to vote his death. There was no telling if he had gained enough ground to sway more than half the council—if, indeed, that mattered at all in the end. Sam Price's vote might be the only one that really counted.

It was a muddy situation, Blaine thought. Like so many such confrontations, more was involved in this than Blaine's guilt or innocence in the minds of these men, his

73

right to invade their sanctuary in quest of personal vengeance. Some might take his side just to buck Sam Price, or, conversely, be afraid to stand up for him because of Price. And the boss of the pack might make his decision for personal reasons that had little to do with Blaine but were concerned rather with his need to reassert his dominance over the devil's legion he had assembled here in these hog-backed hills.

"I knowed Stillwell," Sam Price said thoughtfully. "He stayed here once when he was on the dodge. You don't look like the man who could beat him in a stand-up fight, Blaine."

"I heard of that fight," another council member put in. Sitting behind the table to Blaine's left, he had a mean, scrunched-up face. "Way I heard, Stillwell put two, three bullets into you and you just kept walking in like the wrath of God until you were close enough to blow his head off." The tight, small-featured face creased in an unexpected grin. "That the way it was, Blaine?"

"It exaggerates a little. He hit me once."

"Hell, I'd like to have seen that."

"We could watch it if he went against Seevers," Taggart suggested. "If he's tellin' the truth, he has the right."

"Nobody's said Seevers is here!" Sam Price said sharply.

"Hell, he knows . . ." Taggart's protest trailed off.

"He knows what I want him to know. I told you once, Taggart. Keep your mouth shut."

The flush of anger rose visibly into Taggart's long face. He had a struggle with himself, but in the end caution overruled his pride. The lantern jaw clamped shut, the wide mouth set in a sullen line.

"I don't cotton to no man sets fire to a woman," one of the previously silent council members said slowly.

Price glared at him. "He's under our protection, Sims. That's the rule!" The words ignored Price's own denial that Seevers was present in the camp.

"That's to do with the law—town law." Sims looked at Blaine speculatively. "He ain't wearin' no badge. What's between him and this Seevers is personal. That's different."

"Maybe it is and maybe it ain't."

"I think Seevers lied," the one with the mean-looking monkey's face drawled. "He lied about this Blaine, and he lied about why they both came here."

Sam Price did not refute him. He appeared less belligerent with the other members of the council, bristling only when Taggart appeared to challenge him. Blaine found himself wishing that Taggart would move over to the other side of the argument. Price might rule against him simply because of Taggart.

"We heard enough," Sam Price growled. "This ain't no fence-gossip session. All this palaverin' has made me thirsty, and I got some thinkin' to do." He glanced past Blaine toward the guard at the door. "Shaughnessy, throw him in the *calabozo*."

# EIGHT

Shaughnessy, the big-jawed sentry who had brought Blaine into the camp from the top of the canyon, led him from the meeting hall back through the camp toward the small adobe hut Blaine had noticed earlier. He had little time to see more of the Landing than before, although he did notice a corral and feed barn at the south end of the table that he hadn't seen previously, and what looked like a narrow trail leading along a ledge above the corral and disappearing around the high curve of the main cave. To make note of the track was instinctive. The time might come when he would be looking for an escape hole other than the guarded canyon.

Shaughnessy's manner seemed less hostile after the council session, leading Blaine to question him about its members. The mean-looking man was called Early; he was neither very mean nor a real badman, according to the sentry. He had been a bank clerk tempted into theft, the single crime of his life. The other five were sure-enough bad medicine, Shaughnessy assured Blaine cheerfully. Sims was known to have thrown a wide loop in the cattle business, without regard to the fine points of ownership. Taggart and Olsen were bank robbers, and the other two councilmen, whose names were not given, were among the more notorious gunfighters who had sought temporary residence at Price's Landing. If they elected Blaine to a rope party, the sentry speculated, "Ain't one of 'em will find it a hard pillow to sleep on."

When they reached the tiny *calabozo,* Shaughnessy made it plain that his friendliness wouldn't make him careless. He watched Blaine alertly as he unhooked a rusty padlock and swung open the narrow door on creaking metal. The door was of solid planks, Blaine saw, carried on heavy iron hinges.

"Inside," Shaughnessy said, gesturing with his rifle.

"You think I've got a chance?" Blaine asked.

"Ain't for me to say. Get in."

Blaine, unarmed, recognized the foolishness of attempting to make any break even if he had wanted to. On the unlikely chance that he could overpower the guard, others would be on him in an instant. At least a dozen hardcases were lounging in shade near by, watching him with idle curiosity, every one of them carrying iron. Besides, such a move would defeat Blaine's purpose. He had made his choice when he decided to ride openly into the hideout. Now he could only wait for the council's vote.

As he entered the hut, which was no bigger than an average outhouse, Shaughnessy prodded him hard in the small of his back with his rifle. The move shoved Blaine off balance as the door slammed behind him. The guard wasn't being mean, just practical. It was at the moment when a reckless man faced the interior of a cell that he might balk, suddenly choosing to fight. The feel of a rifle's muzzle ramming into his spine tended to forestall any such action.

Blaine heard the padlock slap into place and close. Then Shaughnessy's steps fell away.

He took stock of his cell. The interior of the adobe enclosure was dark, but not as pitch black as Blaine had expected. From the outside he had noticed no openings at all other than the door. Now he saw that a single mud brick had been left out of one wall at the top for ventilation, another at the bottom for drainage.

The floor was solid rock. The dimensions formed a perfect square, about four feet across. The roof poles, about six feet from the floor on the high side, slanted downward a few inches for runoff, causing Blaine to duck his head on the shorter side. A man could move around the cell easily enough. He could sit with his back propped against a wall and his legs stretched out. He could even curl up on the floor if he got tired enough. He wouldn't be able to stretch out full length, unless he was short enough to get lost in brush.

From the moment the door closed behind him Blaine had become aware of the stifling heat inside the box. Its thick walls would keep it cool enough for the early part of the day, but by this time, well into the afternoon, the long day's heat had turned it into an oven. The two small openings provided little relief. Sweat was instantly running down his cheeks and bathing his body. He noted the fact calmly. Worrying about it wouldn't make the box any cooler.

He sat down, his back against the wall near the bottom opening. Heat rose. If there was any difference at all inside this oven, it would be cooler near the floor.

He wondered how long prisoners were kept here, and what transgressions—other than an uninvited intrusion like his own—might cause a man to be so punished. Certainly a spell in this dark box would tend to discourage the minor quarrels and maverick conduct that didn't merit a bullet or a rope but required some taming. It wouldn't take long confinement on a hot day to temper any man's rebellious streak.

Instead of dwelling on the heat, wondering how long it was until sunset, or speculating vainly over when his fate would be decided, Blaine went carefully over the council meeting. He thought about how men always had to make up rules, whenever enough of them gathered together in one place. It had to be so or you would have every man continually fighting for his place to stand. If that was true among ordinarily law-abiding folks, and it was, then it was doubly necessary in a nest of cutthroats and owl-hooters like Price's Landing. Only the iron rule of a man tougher, meaner, and more dangerous than any other would have enabled the hideout to exist at all in its beginnings. Over the course of time common sense would have forced even a man like that to set down rules, a code of conduct that had to be accepted and obeyed, so that newcomers would know what they could get away with and what would bring instant reprisal. Otherwise Price's Landing would be a smoky place, Blaine thought. Lawless men, banding together, had discovered the necessity of law. He wondered how many of them had ever recognized the irony.

Sam Price had ruled his roost for a long time, Blaine guessed. The cliff dwellings in the back wall of the huge open cave were undoubtedly centuries old, but the crude adobe dwellings of the encampment were almost equally ageless in appearance. Blaine seemed to remember hearing of the Landing four, five years ago. From a one-night stopover camp the hideout had grown into what Price thought of as his "town." He took pride in it. That pride, and the restlessness of men little used to accepting a bit in their mouths, had eventually brought him to accept a degree of communal government, or the pretense of it.

The council. How many of its members had Blaine swayed to his side? Taggart, certainly, if only because he tended to oppose Sam Price. The bank teller, Early, who had heard about the Stillwell fight. And Sims, who had spoken up at the last, pointing out that Blaine didn't wear a badge, that his quarrel with Seevers fell outside the basic rule of the camp that said the entire force of outlaws would stand behind anyone accepted among them. That made three. The others had not committed themselves. Did that mean that they were skeptical of Blaine's story or sympathetic to Seevers' right to sanctuary?

If so, that was three against three.

It all came down to Sam Price, Blaine thought. It probably did, generally, one way or another. It wouldn't be surprising if the outlaw leader had stacked his council that way. And not even Taggart, who hated Price and tried not to let it stampede him, would risk his neck to save Blaine's if Sam Price decided against his claim.

He couldn't change what was going to happen, Blaine thought, with the hard-won patience he had learned over the past eleven months. He felt no regret over the decision to ride into the outlaw camp. Once he let one of Samantha's murderers escape, he would have betrayed her. Her and the boy and himself.

"Sssst!"

Blaine sat up. The hissed whisper had come through the narrow opening at floor level.

"Blaine? You hear me?"

Blaine grunted acknowledgment.

"It's me," the bodiless voice said, stronger now. "Lem Seevers."

Cullom Blaine went cold, all speculation wiped from his mind. He waited, unable to trust himself to answer.

"I know it's you in there. Kinda hot, ain't it?" Seevers chuckled. "Git you ready for where you're goin', Blaine. You'll be in hell soon."

"I'll see you there." Blaine's voice was harsh in his own ears, unrecognizable.

"You ain't never gonna touch me," Seevers retorted angrily. "You ain't never even gonna see me, hear? You can't even prove you are who you told the council, or that I done whatever you claim I done. You don't even know it's true your own self."

Blaine remained silent, reining in the hot wild anger that wanted him to claw at the narrow slot in the wall with his bare hands.

"Listen, you're as good as dead right now," Lem Seevers told him. "You're some kind of a damned fool to follow me to the Landing. You should of knowed better. If you had any sense, you would've." He paused, and Blaine could hear his ragged breathing, as if Seevers were excited by their proximity, afraid and triumphant at the same time. And something else, Blaine thought: guilty as sin. "Listen, it wasn't my idea, what happened to your woman. I had nothin' to do with that part of it at all."

"You did like the others."

"You can't know that."

"Abe Stillwell named you. He named you before he went to hell to hold a place for you."

For a moment Seevers didn't answer. Then he said, "I don't know how you done that. Put Abe down. Hell, ain't no one man could have put Abe Stillwell down. You must of back-shot him."

"You know better," Blaine said coldly. "I shot him fair in the chest, and then blew his head half off."

In the silence that followed Blaine wished that he could see the man beyond the wall, crouching close to the opening, no more than a foot away from him. At least then he could put a face to the man; his hate could be more personal.

"It was Stillwell's idea," Lem Seevers said suddenly, unexpectedly. "Him and those two Clancy boys. They did it to her. I din't have that in my mind at all. You got to believe that, Blaine."

Why? Blaine wondered bitterly. Did the son of a bitch think he could apologize now? That it could all be smoothed over?

"They would of laughed at me if I didn't do like the rest of 'em, like I wasn't as good a man as any," Seevers complained. Blaine wanted to close his ears. He didn't want to listen to Seevers' whining self-defense, or to hear any more details. Yet he could not stop listening as Seevers' voice went on. "You can see we couldn't leave her to talk against us, once it was done. You got to see that. I don't know how you knowed it was any of us at all. She couldn't have told you nothin'. She couldn't of lived through that . . . that burning. Somebody must of talked. Which one was it, Blaine? Which one give you names to save his own neck from stretching? Was it one of them Clancy brothers? Was it Hannifin? Wes Hannifin?"

Blaine said nothing. The nails of his right hand had dug so hard into his palm that he had drawn blood. He welcomed the physical pain.

"What about Brownie? Was he the one? How much did he tell you before you killed him?"

Blaine frowned. Brownie Hayes was another of the Clancy-Stillwell gang, one of those Blaine had sworn to track down if it took him all his days. What did Seevers mean?

"What makes you think Brownie's dead?"

82

"You know goddamn well he's dead! I don't know how you done that, neither. He was holed up down there below the border. I guess he thought he was safe, and you couldn't find him. How did you know where he was? Did *he* tell you where to find me?"

Blaine leaned his head against the wall. He was sorry that someone else had helped Brownie Hayes over the long jump, but he wasn't going to tell that to Lem Seevers. Thinking what he did would only make Seevers more jittery.

"Goddamnit, Blaine, answer me! Say somethin'!"

"You're a dead man, Seevers," he said. He spoke quietly now, like a judge pronouncing sentence. "You burned her alive, and you'll suffer for it before you go. I promise you that."

There was a puzzling, choking sound. After a moment Seevers burst out, enraged, "Do you think you're God? It's Him will punish me for what I done wrong, not you!"

"I'll send you to Him," Blaine said softly.

"No, you won't!" Lem Seevers cried, no longer bothering to keep his voice low so that no one could hear him but the man inside the adobe hut. "They won't let you go, not after what I told 'em about you. Anyways, you'll never know which is me—never. You've lost, Blaine, hear? You've lost!"

"I'm going to offer Price a deal."

"He won't make no deal!"

"Yes, he will," Blaine said, with a confidence he had no reason to feel. "You just think about that. You mean nothing to him, Seevers. Nothing at all."

"God damn you, Blaine!" Seevers choked out, tormented, outraged, afraid. "God damn you all to hell!"

There was a moment's silence, hot and close, before Blaine realized that Seevers was gone.

He sank back against the wall. His mouth felt dry and his heart was pounding. He'd have to learn to control himself better, he thought. He'd have to turn himself into a stone, or one day he'd lose, before he had found them all.

Or was Lem Seevers right? Had he already lost?

# NINE

As a typically foolhardy young man unable to reject a challenge, Cullom Blaine had once allowed himself to be talked into taking part in the purification ceremony at a friendly Kiowa village. There followed four hours in a sweat bath, an experience he had never forgotten—and one which, at the time, he had decided he wouldn't survive. His afternoon in the tiny adobe *calabozo* on Price's Landing brought it all back—the unbearable heat, the oppressive darkness, the stifling air, the rivers of sweat running from every pore and stinging his eyes. If there was a difference, Blaine realized, the Kiowa sweat lodge had indeed been hotter, and for religious reasons it had been totally dark inside, all light shut off except for the red glow of the hot stones on which water was splashed periodically to create fresh steam. But Sam Price's sweat bath would do, Blaine thought. Long before the afternoon waned he found himself hunched close to the floor, not only because the heat was more intense near the roof but also because the faint stirring of air through the brick-size drainage opening at ground level seemed like a cool mountain breeze in comparison with the choking heat of the interior.

The hut stayed hot long after dark. When a tin plate with some strings of beef and beans was shoved through that floor level opening, along with a cup of water, he had to force himself to eat. He chewed each mouthful of food slowly and rationed the water a sip at a time, in spite of the nearly overpowering urge to gulp it down.

If he was going to get out of this situation, he reasoned, he couldn't afford to be sick or weak from hunger and thirst.

After he had eaten he slid the plate and cup back through the slot. He put an eye down to it, but he could see little. He waited a little for his meal to settle, then drove himself through a period of easy, methodical exercise as best he could in that confined space. Sometimes, pausing to listen, he could hear the raucous sounds of rough men relaxing, quarreling over cards or raising their voices in half-drunken contention at the camp saloon. There was even the strumming of a guitar not far away and a singer's doleful lament in a nasal voice. It all sounded incongruously familiar and normal.

Shaughnessy and two other armed guards came for him about two hours after dark. They formed a triangle around him, Shaughnessy in the lead, the other two with rifles behind him on either side. Blaine thought he'd seen surprise in the square-jawed sentry's eyes when Blaine stumbled out of the cell, as if Shaughnessy had expected to have to drag him out and help him to stand. A day in there, Blaine thought, and you'd have to blot me up with your wipes.

The camp was aware of impending drama. Loungers

enjoying the cool evening air on the high table sat up or stood to watch the prisoner as he was led past them. Some called out with jocular gallows humor. "We'll be organizing a string party for you come daylight," one said. "You'll have a neck as long as your nose, bounty hunter, time it's been stretched for you." One bodiless voice observed, "He looks wet through." That set up another man's reply: "We'll hang him up to dry then."

Blaine made no response, although his narrowed eyes searched out faces in the gloom. His jail had been darker, and he found he could see surprisingly well under the open sky, a deep blue sprinkled with early stars. But the faces he saw were all those of strangers. As Seevers' face would be. Was he one of those watching from the shadows? Blaine guessed he was. The guilt and curiosity that had brought him to their low-voiced confrontation at Blaine's tiny cell would surely have Seevers near by to see when Blaine emerged.

He had wondered if Seevers might risk a shot from darkness, the single shot that could end his fears, but nothing happened on the way to the council hall. Probably Seevers knew that it was worth his life to take matters into his own hands before Sam Price and his council made their decision.

The council was waiting. Blaine was escorted to the backless stool in the center and roughly prodded into the seat. The same six men were grouped behind the tables on either side, with Sam Price at the end of the room facing him. Now, however, the hall was crowded with observers, grinning and murmuring asides or scowling balefully at the prisoner. An audience, Blaine concluded, come to watch the fun, as the whole camp would gather in the morning if there was to be a hanging.

Blaine could read nothing in the set faces of the council members. Even those who had seemed to be swayed by his claim, like Taggart, watched him now without expression. Sympathy and pity would have been ominous signs, besides being emotions foreign to such men on the whole. The only thing Blaine had been able to appeal to at all was the Westerner's sense of fair play, a code that often stubbornly persisted even among men who had chosen to ride the high line.

Sam Price commanded silence by banging the butt of his six-shooter on the boards before him. Slowly the room settled down. Then Price read the charge against Blaine: that, for money or personal reasons, he had chased another man to Price's Landing, thus bringing himself under the rules of the town. The man he hunted might or might not be there; if he was, he had placed himself under the protection of Price himself and every other man in the hideout. That was the rule, the first law by which these long riders lived. Against the charge the prisoner had pleaded that the man he pursued had slain his wife, and that no man ought to be entitled to protection for such a crime against the one who had personally been wronged.

Sam Price paused, his one fully open eye peering around the room. There was an excited muttering from the crowd lining the walls, many of whom had not heard Blaine's side of the matter until now. The outlaw leader waited a moment, then banged the gun-butt gavel once more for silence. He looked coldly at Blaine.

"Council votes three for, three against. That leaves it up

to me to decide." Price waited out another swell of excited reaction. "You got anythin' to say, Blaine, before you hear the verdict?"

"He's here," Blaine said. "Seevers come whispering to me outside that sweat lodge of yours. I don't ask any man to side with him or with me. Just turn him out, like you'd turn a rattlesnake out of your own blankets before you'd sleep easy. Turn us both out. It's not your fight, unless you'd care to sidle up to a man who'd jump a decent woman when she was alone and he had six other badmen along to help stiffen his spine." He paused, hating the need to parade what was so personal before these cold-eyed judges. "They boarded her up alive in her own house, and burned it around her. I don't believe Sam Price's gang would want it said they let such a man hide in their shadows."

Sam Price grunted skeptically. "We've only your word on that, and no man here knows you. There's some has ridden with Lem Seevers."

"Then they know him to be a no-good ground crawler, who's scairt to show his face to me, and they'll say the same."

Price did not reply. He was making a ceremony of this mustang court, and Blaine wondered why he was dragging it out. He must have made his decision long ago. Perhaps it had been made for him long before Blaine ever rode into the camp. Price's Landing existed because it offered an outlaw refuge. Could Sam Price allow that sanctuary to be broken, for any reason?

"That all you got to say for yourself, Blaine?"

"If I haven't given you reason enough to turn him out,"

Blaine answered, playing the one card he had left, "then I'll ransom him."

Startled, Sam Price leaned forward to stare at him. Even the drooping hood over his left eye lifted a little. The council members, who had been following the exchange without show of curiosity, as if they already knew the outcome, now sat up alertly. The other onlookers broke into surprised comment, some repeating what Blaine had said to those who hadn't heard him clearly.

"What the hell's that supposed to mean?" Price growled.

"I'll pay whatever price you set on him," Blaine said flatly.

It was a long shot, but he figured he could back up his play. There had been a letter from Tom Wills two months ago in Fort Worth, telling him that he'd succeeded in selling off the new section of land for Blaine. "Land is like gold here," the doctor had written. "There are always buyers, and I believe I have obtained a good price for you, if you agree." Blaine had telegraphed agreement that day. He needed the stake for what he knew was to be a long haul. He would never sell his original land because Samantha was buried there, but the other section meant nothing to him now. It had been a cattleman's purchase when his future had meaning.

"How do you figger to do that?" Price asked finally.

"You set the price on him. I'll send for the money. It could be delivered to McAlister's place, or any other you want to name. Once you have it, you turn Seevers loose. Give him a start, if that's what you think is right. Then let me go after him, and you wash your hands of both of us."

Even before he finished talking, Blaine knew that he had

89

lost his gamble. Several of the council members, even Taggart, who had probably been on his side, were scowling or chewing their lower lips, unhappy or uneasy with Blaine's surprising proposal. Probably most of the men at Price's Landing knew of rewards posted for their capture; the notion of selling out one of their own didn't sit right. Blaine guessed too late that he had turned the mood of the camp against himself, if there had been any doubt before he spoke.

"That's bounty hunter's talk," Taggart said. "I don't like it. I say we vote again, right now."

Sam Price glared at him. "You had your vote. The decision's mine now."

"Let's get on with it, Sam," someone called from the side. "All this listenin' is makin' me thirsty."

There was a mutter of agreement, more openly hostile now. Everyone, including Blaine, knew that the trial was over except for the formalities. He felt nothing, only an emptiness. He didn't fear the outlaws' rope, for in his months on the prod he had come to know in his bones that there was only one way his search could end for himself. A cowman lived close enough to hardship and violence and sudden death to accept it when it came without complaint; a man hunter knew it even better. If a moment of wrenching anguish would come, it would be at that final instant when he knew that he had left some of Samantha's killers go unpunished.

"We don't need your blood money," Sam Price said, after banging his gavel on the table. "But maybe there's one kind of deal could be made." He rode quickly over the startled protests. "It's mine to decide whether you stretch a rope or not," he declared pointedly, his venomous eye silencing the objectors. "What I say is this. We ain't none of us got much likin' for a woman-killer. That's what this Seevers done, and he come crawlin' to us with a lie on his lips, so it ain't like he's got a true claim on us. All the same, what it looks like, Blaine, is you're askin' us to turn him over to you fer a favor, when you ain't done nothin' for us and don't undertake to do anythin', 'ceptin' put up your blood money that we don't want. You goin' along with me so far, Blaine?"

Price was grinning now, a sly grin that made the drooping lid over his left eye look like a conspiratorial wink. Cullom Blaine's eyes glinted with new interest. Price wasn't talking simply because he liked to listen to himself. What was he driving at?

"You got in mind a favor I should do for you?"

"You go straight for the gizzard, Blaine. I like that in a man."

"Hold on, Price!" Taggart protested. "You never said nothin' about this when we was palavering."

"It's my decision," Price repeated harshly. What he said was meant for every man within earshot as well as those who would only hear about the meeting later, but he fixed his hooded stare upon Taggart, with the savvy of a man who knows the best way to quiet a mob is to brace its leader or spokesman, man to man. "I got the say-so to turn this hunter loose, and Seevers with him, like a couple of bobcats in the same gunnysack. That's the way the vote panned out, Taggart. All I'm suggestin' is that we might git something in return." His grin was a nasty curl of his lips. "You questionin' that right?"

Horns locked, Taggart faced up to Sam Price for a long minute. The meeting hall was still. Then Taggart backed off, either because he was afraid or because he saw the logic of Price's claim. "No, it's your vote," he grumbled. "But you might've said something to the rest of us."

"I jest been workin' it out," Sam Price said, his rumbling voice once more sounding amiable. He turned to Blaine. "You see, Blaine, we kinda got us a problem. There's a marshal hereabouts has taken it into his head that he's got a grudge against Price's Landing. He ain't got the sand to ride in here against us, but he's been sittin' outside there, like he's layin' siege against our town. A man ain't free to ride in or out without knowin' he has to go past J. P. Holifield." Some reaction must have shown in Blaine's eyes because Price leaned forward quickly. "You know him?" There was a sharp suspicion in the question.

"I met the marshal. He was at McAlister's when I stopped there."

"Alone?"

"Had a deputy with him, name of Armstrong. And another man who didn't care no more where he went."

"You get a look at that dead man?"

Blaine shook his head, thoughtful now, wondering if he had caught the dangerous drift of Sam Price's thinking. "He was wrapped up end to end. I saw he had red hair, that's all."

Price swore angrily. He looked around the table. The others were more interested in his proposal than before. J. P. Holifield meant something to all of them, something hated and feared, a lawman with a grudge against any of their kind. Some lawmen didn't go out of their way to make war; they acted only when crimes were committed in their own territories. Others, like Holifield, were like sky pilots, preachers with a different sort of crusade against evil, backed by quick guns.

Sam Price said, "I want Holifield put under."

"You got fifty men here, or more," Blaine said slowly. "Why don't you just trample him under yourself?"

The outlaw shook his head. "So far the law's left us alone up here. Maybe 'cuz there's too many of us, maybe 'cuz we're out of the way and there ain't no townfolks liftin' their noses and raisin' their skirts like we was dirt to be swept out of their way. There ain't nothin' Holifield would like better than for a bunch of us to ride out against him. It'd give him excuse to call for help. Before we knew it, we'd have lawmen from a dozen counties and different states and territories gatherin' together to smoke us out of our roost." He paused. "Holifield knows that, and he knows it's why he can sit there on a limb like a goddamn vulture waitin' for the leavings. But if one man was to go against him, it'd be different. Especially if he was a man didn't have anything to do with us, so's they couldn't lay it against Sam Price or any of us here. That man, the one that'd do that, we'd be beholden to him. He could rightly ask us a favor."

The uncrowned ruler of Price's Landing sat back, his good eye fixed unblinkingly on Cullom Blaine. Everyone looked at the prisoner then. Some of the onlookers were whispering eagerly among themselves, sending the word outside to the other curious members of the roost who hadn't been able to crowd inside the hall. A few men grinned openly. Sam Price had come up with an idea no one else had thought of.

Blaine said, "You know I have no reason to go against the law."

Price grinned savagely. "You got one helluva good reason, Blaine. You want Seevers. We'll hold him here for you. Don't worry about that, I already give orders to keep him from flyin' the coop. You do this one thing for us and you get Seevers. You want him so bad it's eatin' your guts out. You do this one thing for us, get Marshal J. P. Holifield off our backs, and Seevers is yours. That's my bargain, Blaine. Take it, and you ride out of here whole. Turn it down, and you'll stretch a rope at first light."

## TEN

The square-jawed Shaughnessy and his sidekick Chico saw Blaine down the canyon to the source of the stream. There they pulled up.

"I never figgered I'd be escortin' you out whilst you was sittin' up straight in the saddle," Shaughnessy said. The statement was without rancor.

"I was kinda doubtful myself for a while."

"That Sam Price, you never know what he's gonna do. He gits some wild notions, Sam does."

Blaine smiled. "You think this is one of 'em?"

"Havin' you tangle with J. P. Holifield?" Shaughnessy grinned. "Ain't no worse than bare-hand rasslin' with a grizzly. That marshal may be considerable smaller, but he's meaner."

Chico nodded sagely. "He is one *malo hombre.*"

"Only one man I can think of I'd hate it worse to have to

tangle with," Shaughnessy said.

"Who might that be?"

"Ol' Sam hisself." The big-jawed outlaw seemed to find this speculation amusing. "You made the right choice, Blaine."

Cullom Blaine said nothing to this. Shaughnessy nodded then, turning his horse's head back up the canyon toward the high table. Chico followed his lead.

"Luck to you, Blaine," Shaughnessy called back.

"Be seeing you."

"Yeah." Shaughnessy chuckled, his skepticism plain. It wasn't clear, however, whether he doubted Blaine's ability to survive the proposed clash with the lawman or simply believed that, given his freedom on Sam Price's whim, Blaine would raise dust all the way to Kansas.

Cullom Blaine turned alone down the narrow stretch of the canyon beside the trickling stream, riding through a cool morning darkness not yet touched by the hot sun already setting the heights afire far above him. He reflected that he hadn't been presented with much of a choice when Sam Price pulled out his surprise in front of the council and the packed audience. The outlaw leader had known that. Blaine had played a loser's hand when he rode into the hideout after Lem Seevers. One way or another he had to get out of Price's Landing alive, even if it meant striking a devil's bargain.

But he couldn't leave it all behind him and run. Not while Seevers lived. Sam Price had shrewdly seen that, too. He saw well enough, Blaine thought, for a man with only one good eye.

What now? Keep his bargain? It went against the grain to

contemplate a deliberate throwdown with Marshal Holifield. It was unthinkable—but he found himself thinking about it as he rode.

Until now his long hunt had been a private matter between himself and the men he pursued. And in the rough justice of that western frontier it would have been accepted as such by most men. It had never brought Blaine up against the law. Yet he had always known that one day it might. His friend Luke Shields, Martinsville's sheriff, had warned him against taking the law into his own hands. "You can't decide it for yourself, Blaine, or first thing you know you'll have the law turned against you instead of them you want to see punished."

"Hannifin and the Clancy brothers didn't hang," Blaine had said. "And the law hasn't touched the others."

Shields, a sympathetic and troubled man, had sighed. "I know how you feel, but I wouldn't want to see a reward dodger come across my desk with your name on it. It wouldn't seem right. That's not the way to put things right for Mrs. Blaine."

"What way would do it, Sheriff?"

Only one, Blaine answered his own question now. To see the men who had murdered her pay as bitter a price.

Everyone seemed bent on making him see the light that bringing about that justice wasn't his to do. The law would find and judge and sentence the guilty, Luke Shields had argued. But the law was busy, the law demanded formalities of evidence that Blaine didn't need, and after a while the law forgot. And no law reached into a place like Price's Landing, or any of a hundred such holes into which Seevers and the others might dive and hide. God would judge and punish him, Lem Seevers himself had cried out. Well, God had been looking the other way when Samantha was condemned to her hour of hell on earth. Maybe God was busy, too. Right or wrong, Blaine couldn't leave it up to Him.

Kneeling in the soot beside his gutted house, with the blackened thing that had been his wife cradled in his arms, as light as a floating ash, Cullom Blaine had made a simple vow. Until he had run every last one of Samantha's killers to earth, nothing would block him from keeping that promise.

Nevertheless, he had never before faced the necessity of killing a man against whom he had no personal grudge or grievance. Could he bring himself to do it, even to keep his vow? The question had shaken him, making his last night in Sam Price's stronghold a sleepless one.

Was there another way? He might try to wait Seevers out. Eventually Seevers would tire of his refuge with the outlaw gang, especially now that his story was known. Not many crimes would ostracize a man among Sam Price's cutthroat crew. Cattle rustling, horse stealing, robbery, even murder were accepted. But there were deeds that were despised even among the worst outlaws. Backshooting a partner was one. Raping, torturing, and murdering a decent woman was surely another. Seevers wouldn't find himself welcome among his own kind. Sooner or later, if he was allowed to and thought it safe, he would make another run.

But time wasn't something Blaine could spend lavishly. Time gave the others a longer rope, a chance for their trails to turn colder. Waiting for one man too long, Blaine might lose all the others. That was a risk he couldn't accept.

Could he have another try at invading Price's Landing? Over those trackless wastes to the south, might there not be another way to climb to those ancient caves Sam Price had discovered?

Blaine had been given a semblance of freedom in the camp after he had agreed to Sam Price's deal, and he had tried to impress on his mind as many details about the hideout as he was able to observe. But at night the darkness had limited his scouting, and that morning he had been closely watched. What he had learned was not encouraging. The ancient Indians who had first settled there centuries ago had chosen the site deliberately because it was so inaccessible, its few approaches easily watched and defended. Sam Price had had plenty of time to make the place virtually impregnable against the attack even of a small army, much less one man trying to break in unseen.

There was only one possibility, a remote one. Blaine had seen portions of an old Indian foot trail leading away from the caves. That track led not toward the canyon exit but away from it, disappearing into the hills south of the Landing. It might lead nowhere. After untold years of erosion and weathering, that narrow path might have been worn away, covered by landslides, cut off by new fissures in the changing hills. If, on the other hand, it was known to be still passable, Sam Price might have it watched, even though it wasn't wide enough to admit one man on horseback.

A thin chance, Blaine thought. Not impossible, but long odds. Longer than he wanted to give Lem Seevers, for Blaine knew that if he were caught sneaking back into the camp he would be killed without hesitation. The council wouldn't need to vote on it.

Would J. P. Holifield listen to reason? Would he go along with a plan to make Sam Price *think* the marshal had been chased off? Remembering Holifield's suspicious, hostile appraisal of a passing stranger, Blaine doubted that he would listen. And it was equally doubtful that Price could so easily be fooled. He might insist on some proof that Blaine couldn't give.

Unless he did what the outlaw demanded as his part of the bargain.

Restless, uneasy with the decision he had to make, Cullom Blaine rode out of the morning shadows at the bottom of the deep cleft into bright sunlight that narrowed his eyes to slits.

A mile away across the stony flats that reached to another line of slab-sided hills, another pair of eyes squinted through a pair of bring-'em-close glasses toward the south. His gaze moved down the tall pink column of the singing tower that clearly marked the trail leading to the canyon entrance to Price's Landing. Their line of view reaching the bottom of the tower, the field glasses stopped suddenly. The eager young deputy who was holding them sighted in as closely as he could on the mounted figure emerging from the shadowed hills.

Tom Armstrong slapped one hand against the rock shelf on which he lay in a patch of shade. He recognized the rider. He was the same man who had ridden into McAlister's place a few days earlier, bold as brass, when Armstrong and the marshal had been there. He had called himself Blaine. Holifield had pegged him right after all!

There had been something about the man that stayed in

Tom Armstrong's mind even after so brief a meeting. He wasn't the kind of man you could ignore, but the deputy wasn't sure what it was that had struck him so forcibly. It was a quality that told Armstrong this man would ride right over you if you tried to stand in his way, but he couldn't have said what gave rise to the impression or made it stick in his memory. Blaine hadn't blustered or shown any special belligerence. He had been quiet, soft-spoken, at ease with himself.

Maybe that was it, Armstrong thought. He had been too cool and steady. The stillness in him was a warning.

Marshal Holifield had expressed the belief that Blaine was on the dodge. Soon as they got to town he had spent an hour going through the stack of posters and letters and reports in his desk. Then he'd fired off a couple of telegrams the same day. Tom Armstrong didn't know what Holifield might have learned since then, for the deputy had been ordered back to his scouting mission, which found him now tracking the man called Blaine with his glasses as he swung east, turning away from the regular trail, riding without haste. What was he up to?

No matter. The important thing was that old J.P. had been proved right once more. He could smell out a hair-trigger man like a bird dog flushing quail. "He's a killer," Holifield had asserted with flat conviction. "It's in his eyes. I've seen too many of 'em to mistake the look."

Armstrong had noticed Blaine's eyes. They were brown with vivid green flecks, bright in his sun-dark face; you couldn't help remarking them. But the deputy admitted to himself that he hadn't seen murder there. He lacked the marshal's long experience with such men, but damned if he wasn't learning fast!

He lost the distant rider behind an intervening ridge. He put down the glasses. Excitement made him jittery, and he was sweating heavily. He dragged a sleeve across his damp brow and used his wipes to dry the sweatband inside his hat. He was thinking hard. He was supposed to report back to McAlister's spread that night or the following morning. The marshal would meet him there. But should he wait?

No, this was something Holifield would want to know. Blaine had ridden into Price's Landing, and he had come out untouched. Only a man of the outlaw breed could do that. The story Blaine had told about following someone had sounded plausible enough to Armstrong, although the marshal had brushed it aside. Well, it didn't hold any more water now than a lace handkerchief.

With abrupt decision Armstrong scrambled up, slipped his field glasses into their leather case, and slid down from his ledge. In that moment the decision that Cullom Blaine was grimly pondering was taken out of his hands.

Unaware of being watched, Blaine picked his way slowly across the sun-blasted wilderness that surrounded and pro- tected Sam Price's craggy retreat. He was searching out the land, looking for other ways to climb or circle south as well as other routes that might lead out of this broken country to the east or to the north, where Asahel McAlister's ranch lay beyond some distant hills. At the same time he was trying to find a way out of the dilemma in which his own quest and Sam Price's canniness had placed him. He felt like a gopher trapped underground, with someone up above closing off all the exit holes but one.

He had no way of knowing that his own hard choice no longer mattered, that what would come had been inevitable since the moment he had returned J. P. Holifield's sharp scrutiny with a steady gaze that was cool, indifferent, and without fear.

# ELEVEN

Blaine camped that night in barren foothills nearly a day's ride north of Price's Landing and a similar distance from McAlister's valley, a halfway spot that seemed to suggest his uncertainty of mind. Yet he had come to a conclusion of sorts, reluctantly. The law would have one more chance. He would seek Holifield out. If the marshal was as hell-bent for justice as his reputation suggested, he might co-operate.

Blaine had little real hope for such an outcome, but a day's lonely pondering had led him to the conclusion that he had to give it a try. After that . . . well, the outlines of what lay ahead were already beginning to take shape, how-ever vaguely. Shooting the lawman without cause was not part of it. That meant that he had to ride around Price's mountain and find the bottom of that Indian track. It stood to reason that the first builders of that refuge in the heights wouldn't have left themselves with only one track to follow. They must have had an exit hole, as any smart animal did. Blaine would have to find it.

He slept more at ease under the stars that brightened a clear sky.

The land seemed empty. On the high peaks and tables and ridges, painted white along their upper surfaces by the early moon, nothing moved. Even down in the tortuous ravines and splits among the hills, or in the shadows of the dry arroyos that cut across the lower flats, the night was still and silent, empty even of the scurryings of nocturnal animals or the quick, erratic flapping of bats rising from their dark holes.

The middle hours of the night passed, the slender moon was gone, and the sprinkling of stars winked out, one by one. In the deeper blackness of the last hour before dawn, the trap was set.

Cullom Blaine rose early, refreshed by his few hours of sleep. His movements were economical, unhurried, the actions of a man who had lived close to the land for a long time, as Blaine had always done, especially during this past year in the saddle. He built a small fire quickly and heated coffee. The fire was for the coffee only, for he ate a light cold meal. Like most men who had ridden the cattle trails of this harsh country, his coffee was important to him. He liked it hot and black and strong, and plentiful. By the time he had scalded his throat sufficiently to burn away any lingering dullness from sleep, thrown the last dregs onto the fire and stamped out the embers, scuffing dirt over the ashes with his boots, he was wide awake and alert.

He saddled his buckskin and threaded his way through some raw, eroded foothills toward the trail that led north. He had deliberately chosen a campsite well away from any beaten track, hidden in one of the hundreds of tiny clefts that etched these hills like the cut teeth of a saw, but he meant to ride openly into McAlister's valley.

He had not forgotten the lifeless cargo J. P. Holifield had

been escorting that day at McAlister's.

A morning's steady riding brought him to the crest of one of a series of high ridges he had to cross. From there he wound through a line of sculptured hills, smoothed and rounded by the winds and rains of countless centuries. He skirted those pockets and creases he could avoid, rode watchful when he had to cross naked flats or swing past screening patches of brush or cedar brakes. He saw nothing amiss. Yet a feeling of uneasiness began to nudge at him, claiming attention without reason. It was a feeling that would not go away, and one that he could not ignore.

Cullom Blaine had survived a bitter war, and lived through a dozen years on the frontier. He had come out of Indian raids and fights with only some nicks and creases, the kind of marks that anything living or dead in this raw land acquired with time. He had felt fists and boots in brawling towns that cropped up beyond the push of the law, and he had faced more than one man's angry guns. As a cowman he had pulled through floods and droughts and stampedes. He had grown to be a careful man, keenly attuned to the land he had come to love when there was room in him for love. Now he felt that he was not alone in the empty land, that he was being watched, that danger, never completely absent, was close and real.

Indians? He had seen old tracks of unshod ponies that morning, but none that were fresh. He had seen no quick dust, no unidentified movement. He had surmised that Sam Price might have him followed, but in his scouting of the hills and canyons east of Price's Landing through most of the previous day he had satisfied himself that no one dogged his tracks.

Yet there was something. . . .

In the late morning a switchback trail brought him to a high pass between two peaks as tall as any he had to breach this day. When the way opened out he found himself overlooking a natural bowl. The trail dropped suddenly to the bottom, a grassy meadow little more than a hundred feet below the heights, and less than two hundred yards across. This table was cupped by steep cliffs or rocky bluffs all around, their walls canting slightly inward like the sides of a bowl or cup. At the far side the walls dipped low and the trail cut through a split that was like a spillway.

But what claimed Blaine's attention was not these details but the burned grass across two thirds of the meadow. He remembered it from his last passage this way, heading south. At that time the burned patch had made him think of Apaches. Now he wondered. A grass fire could start from a hundred causes. This one had cleared the area where the trail wound, denuding it of cover.

Pausing at the south rim, Blaine studied the scene, his gaze alert as it traveled along the irregular lines of the surrounding hills, cut sharply against the blue of the sky. A hot breeze blew steadily, sometimes in strong puffs, but it carried to him no warning scent of dust or man or horse.

At length he shrugged and started down. Across the burned floor of the meadow he rode slowly, letting Randy pick his own pace. Blaine's uneasiness grew heavier, a pressure he could feel against his spine and the back of his neck. If he had been hunter or hunted that morning, instead of a man riding to seek the law's help, he would have hesitated longer over dipping into this bowl.

Near the far side of the scorched meadow, where the trail

funneled toward the notch in the rocky bluffs, Blaine saw a sudden spurt of dust just ahead. He pulled up sharply as the echoing whack of a rifle reached his ears.

The spray had kicked up about ten feet in front and to his right, but the sound had come from somewhere behind him. Somewhere on the heights overlooking the bowl.

A poor shot, or a warning one. Blaine guessed the latter. For that reason he pulled up instead of making a run.

"That's sensible, Blaine," a voice called out. Its thin rasp drifted clearly to him from the rock cover directly ahead. "Come ahead, same as you were."

Blaine kneed the buckskin into a walk. Twenty feet from the nearest rocks the unseen voice commanded him to stop.

"Close enough. Unhitch your belt, Blaine. Slow and easy. You move sudden and you're done. That's fine. Now let her drop."

The metal in the gun butt clattered against a small rock when Blaine dropped his belt to the ground. Blaine sat motionless then, his narrowed eyes expressionless, his face a mask. He was not to be shot out of the saddle, he thought. At least not yet.

"Keep your hands on the saddlehorn, mister. I got a bead on your ribs, so don't try to skin that rifle."

"What's this all about, Marshal?" Blaine felt cold anger rising. There was no mistaking that voice, although he had heard it only once before.

"You'll learn, soon enough."

Blaine waited in silence. After a few moments he heard the clop of hoofs approaching behind him as a rider crossed the brown meadow. That would be the owner of the rifle that fired the warning shot, he thought. The trap had been neatly set, made easy by the terrain and its victim's carelessness. Well, the marshal could apologize later.

But Holifield hadn't caught him by mistake. He had called out his name.

The tiny crease of a frown was the only visible reaction in Blaine's face. He sat comfortably in the saddle, his wide shoulders relaxed, waiting without impatience for the rider at his rear to cover the ground between them. He had waited longer for more important things.

The rider moved level with him, a safe five yards to his right. Blaine flicked a glance that way without turning his head. He recognized Holifield's young deputy. Armstrong's eager, unmarked face revealed his excitement. His lips were parted over even white teeth, and his eyes were too bright. Hell, the marshal must be hard put for deputies if he had to go cradle robbing, Blaine thought. There was a wry chagrin in the reflection, for he had not seen Armstrong when he rode by him.

Blaine's gaze jerked back to the slot dead ahead as Marshal Holifield stepped into view. He had been on foot up in those rocks. His hostile gaze speared Cullom Blaine briefly. Then he turned and disappeared. A moment later Blaine heard the rub and squeak of a rig and the marshal rode a chestnut gelding onto the trail.

"Get his belt and his rifle," Holifield told the deputy.

"Hold on." Blaine's tone was quiet, but it held a warning. "You've no call to jump me like this. I've broken no law."

"That's to be seen," the marshal snapped back. "I wouldn't expect you to say different. You heard me, Armstrong. You want to give him any trouble, Blaine, go right ahead. You'll just make things easier all around."

"Meaning you'd just as soon take me in in a canvas roll."

"I don't much care one way or the other," Holifield said coldly.

"That way's easier than waiting for a trial, or trying to make loose charges stick."

He saw Holifield's thin mouth tighten behind his drooping brown mustache. When he had been afoot Holifield's small size had been more apparent. A horse was a different kind of equalizer, Blaine thought, bringing most men closer to level when they were in the saddle. There was the small man's bristling feistiness about the lawman. But Blaine had known other bantam roosters who broke into cackling laughter as easily as they took offense. The hostility in J. P. Holifield's sharp eyes spoke of something deeper. Blaine couldn't imagine those thin lips relenting, or those icy eyes melting into warmth. He had thought of a preacher when he'd met Holifield the first time, and he did again. Not any kind of preacher, but the kind that was full of righteousness, devoid of humor.

It occurred to Blaine that some men might make the same charge against him. It hadn't always been that way. Once he had been a man quick enough to grin or joke, with the rough, ready humor men used on the frontier to soften the hazards and hard challenges of their daily lives, making light of danger or hardship by belittling it. In the past year, however, laughter had come as seldom to his lips as it must to Holifield's.

The men were silent until Armstrong had picked up Blaine's gun belt and slicked his rifle from its scabbard. When the deputy had withdrawn once more to a safe distance the marshal said, "You'll get your trial, Blaine."

"Just what am I accused of?"

"You rode out of Price's Landing yesterday. That's good enough for me."

"I told you why I had to go there."

"Yeah, I heard your tale. You find the man you was supposed to be hunting?"

"Give me a chance and I'll tell you that, too. I was meaning to, anyway. That's why I was heading back to McAlister's place."

Holifield snorted. "I checked on you, Blaine, if that's who you are. The word is that you used to be a stand-up man until your wife got herself killed. Since then you've turned killer."

"If that's what you call shooting varmints."

"You gunned Abe Stillwell down over at Fort Smith."

"It was a fair fight."

Holifield's lips curled behind their brush. That must be the nearest thing to a grin that sharp mouth knew, Blaine thought. "That makes you some kind of a he-wolf, don't it, Blaine? You'd have to be that to take a hellion like Stillwell in a stand-up fight. Funny, you don't look so tough right now. I'd guess Deputy Armstrong here could make you roll over and wave your legs."

Blaine said nothing. What was happening didn't make sense. No charges had been brought against him for the Stillwell shooting. There had been too many witnesses for any doubt to be raised.

"Trouble is, you didn't shoot Brownie Hayes over in El Paso in a fair fight, Mr. He-Wolf. You wrung his neck."

"I don't know what you're talking about."

Blaine's eyes slitted as he listened to Holifield's unexpected accusation. He was remembering Lem Seevers' puzzling words about Brownie Hayes. Seevers had also believed that Blaine had killed the man.

"You know. Hayes was running with the Stillwell-Clancy bunch. That would put him on your balance sheet, Blaine. He turned up dead in a crib over there along the border, with a little Mex girl screamin' her head off. They din't catch you at it, but I reckon the sheriff there will want to have a talk with you when he hears I've got you behind bars where you belong."

"I wasn't in El Paso this past year. I didn't kill Hayes, and I'm sorry to hear he's dead." Blaine meant what he said. He didn't want any of them to buy his ticket before he had found them all. "But if I had done it, it would have been because he deserved killing."

"You're not the law!" Holifield snarled. A sudden, dangerous rage gripped him. He rode his chestnut closer. Blaine saw that the marshal's narrow-chested frame was quivering like a bow bent to its limit, ready to snap. "You're no better than the other killers—you're out of the same button box. You think you can make your own law, and you don't need no badge. You'll decide your own self who's worth killing and who's to be allowed to go on breathin'. Well, no man-killer runs loose in my territory, Blaine. If that's who you are, if Blaine is your name and you went into Price's Landing after another man, he'd have to be one of the same gang you're hunting, and you wouldn't have come out unless he was dead. That's reason enough for me to take you in. That is, unless the whole tale is a pack of lies. I reckon there's plenty of gun-slicks like you would lay claim to be the man that put Abe Stillwell

110

on his back. That'd make you ride taller, wouldn't it? Whichever it is, your killing days are done." Savagely the marshal jerked his horse's head around, facing north. "You ride ahead of us, Deputy."

"Those men you talk about—"

"Save your breath, Blaine! You'll need it when you're wearin' a rope for a choke strap."

The lawman turned away from Blaine's unfinished protest. He took his place behind Blaine's horse while the deputy rode in front of them. For a moment Blaine fought to get his anger under rein. Then he felt the buckskin stir as Armstrong started forward. Blaine let Randy follow.

There had been something wild in J. P. Holifield's outburst, something unreasoning, as if the man himself were aware of the weakness of his arguments, although Blaine doubted that he was. He had seen enough of the marshal to recognize the fanatic's conviction. Holifield was a man who, far from acting in a way that he felt was wrong, or evil, was absolutely sure of the rightness of everything he did. He had made his judgment of Blaine, and it simply didn't enter his head that he could be wrong. At their first meeting he had taken an instant dislike to Blaine, who had sensed it at the time, but Holifield would never acknowledge to himself that his judgment might have been affected by that immediate hostility, the reaction of one headstrong man encountering another.

Probably J. P. Holifield didn't much care if Blaine had spoken the truth or not, or even if he was the man he claimed to be. As far as the marshal was concerned, if Blaine was in fact the man from Martinsville, then he was a self-acknowledged killer, embarked on a trail of

111

vengeance across Texas that had brought him into Holifield's territory. The lawman's instinct for protecting from poachers what he regarded as the law's prerogative would compel him to stop such an intruder. If, on the other hand, Blaine had lied, if he was just another of Sam Price's owl-hoot bunch, then he wasn't worth a second thought. Either way, J. P. Holifield's mind was set, open to no question. The arguments he used were only words he grabbed at to justify what he already believed, which was simply that this man who called himself Blaine had already punched his ticket to hell and J. P. Holifield was there to see him on his way, as was his duty. He would sleep soundly, Blaine guessed, when it was done.

If Blaine had tried to make a fight of it back there in the scorched bowl, or if now he tried to run and Holifield or the smooth-cheeked deputy shot him in the act, the marshal would feel himself justified—would even say that he had been proven right. It was one man's law, Blaine thought, the kind he himself had vowed to carry out.

But there was a difference. Blaine had been reluctant, finally unwilling to turn his guns against a man who had done him no wrong. Holifield felt no such hesitancy. His badge, and his self-righteous nature, armed him against it.

Dropping into a shadowed cleft that penetrated the last line of hills between the string of riders and Asa McAlister's valley, Cullom Blaine felt a chill of warning coinciding with the momentary loss of the sun. He thought again of that young renegade whose death had touched Iris McAlister so deeply, and of the other unidentified outlaw Blaine had seen wrapped in his ground sheet.

*That's what he plans,* Blaine thought. *He doesn't mean*

*for me to go before any judge.*

J. P. Holifield had already tried him. Somewhere between these hills and the marshal's town jail, his sentence would be carried out.

# TWELVE

For the last hour the three riders, crossing the broad valley at a pace slowed to a crawl by the punishing heat, sighted their course on a thin plume of smoke that curled upward from Asa McAlister's ranch house. On a day this hot it had to be from the fire in a cooking stove. The sun dropped behind smoke-blue hills and the western sky shaded from red to orange to a paler pink. The colors of the land changed swiftly. The hills darkened into purple mystery. The broad sweep of grassland turned a duller brown. For a time long shadows etched the Cinders to the north into sharply outlined bluffs and towers. Then these were enveloped in the softer hues of evening, as the cooking smoke disappeared into the rising gray of dusk, and the darkness welled up from the pockets in the hills to reach the highest peaks, turning them black against the lingering light in the sky.

Of the three men only the one in the middle noticed. The beauty of the land and the exhilaration of its limitless spaces acquired a heightened appeal for a man about to find his freedom limited to the dimensions of a jail cell.

Lanterns inside the buildings made yellow oblongs of the bunkhouse door and the windows of the ranch house as the riders drew near. Some of McAlister's hands drifted out to watch them in silent curiosity. The white-haired rancher stepped down from his porch to meet Marshal Holifield, who had trotted forward as the riders reached the yard. Blaine saw McAlister's young wife in the doorway of the house. The light behind her made a halo of her golden hair. She wore a long-sleeved calico dress, full-skirted but snug around her slender waist. There were tiny flowers scattered over the lavender fabric. She made a pretty picture in her frame of yellow light.

Blaine jerked his gaze away, wondering why he had noticed her in such detail. Or was the reason similar to his sudden awareness of the beauty of a sunset, an awareness born of loss?

"Evening, Marshal. Armstrong . . . Blaine. You're just in time for supper." McAlister took note of the fact that Blaine wasn't wearing his gun belt, that his rifle scabbard was empty. He frowned. "Somethin' wrong, Mr. Holifield?"

"Nothin' that ain't bein' put right," the lawman answered. "The deputy and me'd be obliged for a hot meal. I reckon maybe my prisoner's hungry, too, if you'd care to feed him."

"Isn't that Mr. Blaine?" McAlister was puzzled. He had thought Blaine a quiet, steady sort, not the kind J. P. Holifield usually brought in under the prod of a rifle.

"It's what he calls himself," Holifield said, swinging down.

"I don't understand, Marshal. Surely he has done nothing—"

"He's a wanted man," the lawman said curtly as he loosened the cinch under the mare's belly. "I figgered as much when I saw where he was headed the other day."

Iris McAlister was still standing in her open doorway, staring across the yard at Blaine. She had her back to the light and he couldn't read her expression. He wondered if there was concern or worry in those blue eyes. Such details not being visible, there was nothing to mar the pretty picture.

"Soon as we turn our horses loose," the marshal said, "I'd like to hobble my prisoner. You still got that lock and chain handy?"

McAlister nodded. His gaze shifted uncomfortably away from Blaine, but it kept wanting to come back, as if he hoped to find in the silent man's face the answer to his puzzlement.

While Holifield followed the tall rancher, Blaine and Armstrong let the three horses drink, then led them over to the corral. Blaine stripped off Randy's rig under the deputy's watchful gaze. When Armstrong ordered him to do the same for the other two horses, Blaine said curtly, "Do it yourself." The deputy looked angry but unsure. The deadlock was broken by Brazos Bill, McAlister's oversized cowpoker, who was holding up a corral post near by. He took care of the lawmen's mounts.

By the time Armstrong had marched Blaine back across the yard, J. P. Holifield was waiting with a length of heavy chain and a big padlock in his hands. He put the chains on Blaine himself. He did it roughly, and he enjoyed what he was doing. He also seemed to enjoy the fact that McAlister and his wife were watching from the long porch. With Armstrong holding the muzzle of his rifle aimed at Blaine's middle, the marshal hauled him over to the stone lip of a well that rose two feet above the ground. He forced his prisoner to sit. Then he wrapped a length of the chain around Blaine's legs above the ankles, jerking the overlapping circles cruelly tight. He ran the chain around one of the cover posts of the well and secured it with the heavy padlock, joining links of the two ends of the chain. He had kept the connecting chain as short as possible.

Ankle-tied like that, Blaine had very little play. He could shift his body around on the ground freely, but his legs and feet were more or less anchored in place by the short chain. The position was uncomfortable, but more than that it was humiliating, just as Holifield intended.

Blaine saw that J. P. Holifield could smile after all. He stood over Blaine when it was done, keeping just out of reach, and stared down at him. Behind the stained brown mustache a thin smile appeared. It wasn't much of a smile, nor a very pleasant one, but it meant the same as any other. It said that the man who wore it was enjoying himself.

Holifield must have been waiting for Blaine to shout or curse or rage at him. When Blaine said nothing, merely sat in the dust with his shoulder against the cool stone parapet of the well, the marshal's grin faded away. He stalked off to the house. Blaine heard his boots stamp up the steps and across the porch. Door hinges creaked.

He did not look up. A moment later Armstrong followed his boss into the house and Blaine was left alone. That is, he might as well have been alone. A few of McAlister's ranch hands were idling in front of the bunkhouse, smoking and talking, but no one came near J. P. Holifield's prisoner. Most hands, for all their Saturday night reputations as hell-raisers, were peaceable men who gave trouble a wide berth unless it was forced on them. Blaine was trouble.

After a while Blaine heard the door to the ranch house open and close. The step on the porch this time was light. Iris McAlister's long skirt rustled as she crossed to the well. She had brought a plate of food and coffee. Blaine was both hungry and thirsty, and he knew better than to let anger get in the way of nourishment. He wasn't finished yet. He meant to have a try at those chains sometime during the night. Meanwhile he had better take whatever food and rest he could get.

The young woman handed him the plate and cup in silence, her gaze averted. She started to turn away, hesitated, looked back. Then she spoke, her voice pitched low.

"What have you done, Mr. Blaine?"

"To earn these chains?"

"Yes."

"Nothing."

"I can't believe that. The marshal wouldn't . . ."

"I think you can believe it. Because you know he would."

She faced him then directly, her eyes meeting his in a searching gaze, and she realized that she did believe him. She wasn't certain why, for her fear and hatred of Marshal Holifield didn't explain it completely. Nor did she understand the sympathy this hard, embittered man aroused in her. He wasn't anything like Edward Coleman, the towheaded boy her heart had gone out to, a happy-go-lucky youth close to her own age. But instinct had told her the first night Blaine had stopped at the ranch that he wasn't like the cat-eyed men who had passed before him on their way south, any more than he resembled young Coleman.

"You said once you were the same as those others, the men of Price's Landing."

Blaine remembered, and he made no protest. Instead he sampled the slab of beef she had brought. It was tender enough to cut with a fork.

"Are you an outlaw, then?"

"No, ma'am."

"Mr. Holifield thinks you are."

"He wants to think it."

"Yes . . . that's how it would be, wouldn't it?" She seemed to be agreeing with herself, thoughtfully verifying a previous assumption. "Did you find the man you were following?"

"He's there. I wasn't allowed to find him."

"I see." She was silent a moment. Her glance strayed toward the house, as if she feared that someone would soon come looking for her, wondering why she took so long with the prisoner. "What did he do to you, Mr. Blaine?"

He made no reply. She studied his face in the darkness, sensing rather than seeing its hard cast, realizing that her question had reached the unyielding barrier she felt in the man. Suddenly her intuition told her why she believed him different from Sam Price's equally hardened outlaws. What drove Cullom Blaine was not greed or recklessness or a wild streak, or the killing meanness that was in some men on both sides of the law. The force in Blaine was pain. Something brooded deep inside him, like an old grief. She wondered what part the man he pursued had played in that buried hurt, but she knew that he would never tell her.

Yet she asked, surprising herself. "Was it a woman?"

Startled, Blaine answered harshly. "Let it alone, Mrs.

McAlister." He held out his plate to her, no longer hungry.

The porch door creaked, and a tall figure filled the yellow rectangle of the doorway. McAlister's mane of white hair brushed the top of the door frame. "Iris?" he called out.

"I'll be right along, Mr. McAlister." She refused to take Blaine's half-empty plate, but said very clearly, "There's more if you're still hungry, Mr. Blaine. And more coffee, too."

Blaine watched her cross the yard and enter the house. McAlister held the door for her, then stood for a moment, peering toward the man chained to the well. It worries him as well, Blaine thought. They were decent people, both of them, caught in the middle. But there was nothing they could do for him.

J. P. Holifield would have to be careful about raising too many questions in people's minds, he thought. Or was the marshal's reputation so secure, his hold on his territory so strong, that he didn't need to be concerned about what right-thinking people whispered behind his back?

The links of the chain that tied Blaine to the well were a full inch across. The well post to which the chain was attached seemed solid, as did the cross bar that joined two posts so that the chain could not simply be lifted clear. The coils around his ankles were so tight that they seemed to offer little hope that he could skin out of them. He would try, of course, but that would come later, when it was dark and quiet, and everyone slept. The only thing in his favor was the fact that the marshal apparently felt that his prisoner was safely trussed up for the night.

When his plate was empty Blaine set it on the stone ledge beside him and finished his coffee. He felt the urge for a cigarette and found the makings in his shirt pocket. He rolled a cigarette carefully, licked the paper, stuck it in a corner of his mouth. Then he found that he had nothing to light it with. His flint box and matches were both in his war bag. With a shrug he tossed the unlighted cigarette away.

He made himself as comfortable as he could. There was iron in him, and it showed in the patience that kept him from raging or protesting or wasting his strength in futile struggles. His chance would come.

He wondered what J. P. Holifield had planned for him, but he realized this speculation was useless and abandoned it.

A short while later, surprisingly, he slept.

# THIRTEEN

Waking suddenly, Blaine was almost instantly alert, listening. The sky was deep and clear, with some cloud patches. One of these was trailing an edge across the face of the moon, softening its light as a shade softened a lamp's flame. The house and barn and sheds and bunkhouse were all dark. Down in the corral a horse or two stirred, but most stood placid. A light cool breeze touched Blaine's cheek, but it was not enough to awaken a clattering of loose shutters or a rustling of debris adrift across the dusty yard. Not enough to wake him. And the shadows all around seemed fixed and natural.

Then the cloud shouldered in front of the moon. In the deeper blackness Blaine saw something move. He sat up quickly. The shape flowed away from a corner of the ranch house and glided soundlessly toward him. Only when she drew quite close did he recognize the pale oval of Iris McAlister's face.

She knelt beside him. She had a scarf or mantle of some sort over her head to hide her hair, which always seemed to catch whatever light was about.

"What are you—?"

"Shhh!"

She fumbled with the heavy, rusty padlock. Blaine felt a leap of hope. Hearing her gasp of frustration when the lock resisted her, he took it from her. She had brought the key. Blaine gave it a sharp twist. The loop of steel kicked open.

Loosening and shucking off his chains, slowly and carefully to avoid any more rattling than necessary, Blaine didn't ask how she had obtained the key, or why.

When he was free, he rubbed ankles chafed raw by the heavy iron coils. He hadn't got over his surprise, and he was fumbling for words of gratitude.

"You'd better hurry," Iris McAlister whispered.

"You're taking a hell of a chance."

Her head shook in denial. "My husband will protect me. He's too well known and liked for the marshal to act against me, even if he found out."

Blaine wondered if that was true, but he couldn't deny her faith. "Your husband's a lucky man," he said softly.

She stared at him for a moment, her expression drawn and troubled, strangely yearning. Then she seemed to shake herself. "You can't go near the corral," she whispered urgently. "The marshal has posted his deputy there."

"He might be asleep."

"You'd wake him. I couldn't get you your horse, but you'll find a mare down by the creek, near those big twin

121

cottonwoods, saddled and ready. She isn't your buckskin, but she's a good horse, and strong enough to carry you."

"How'd you manage all that?" Blaine asked, marveling at her.

"One of the men did it for me. Mostly they'll do anything I ask, and he won't talk."

Remembering how the crew had behaved around her, Blaine believed her. "Do you have a gun?" he asked.

"No. I'm sorry."

"Don't be. You've done all you could, and more than I could ask."

"I don't know why, Mr. Blaine."

After a moment's pause he said, "Maybe because you'd give any man a fair chance."

His big hand closed over her shoulder, squeezed once. Then he was gone.

She watched him glide across the yard. He crouched low but he moved with surprising speed. When he started down the slope toward the stream she lost him in the ground shadows.

Reluctantly she walked back to the porch and stood there, staring after Blaine long after he had disappeared. At length she sighed and stepped onto the porch.

From the darkness at the far end came a soft chuckle.

A chill of alarm squeezed a gasp from her. From the deep shadows J. P. Holifield appeared. He walked soundlessly, and she realized that he was not wearing his boots. Without them he seemed even shorter than usual. Their eyes met at the same level.

In sudden panic she turned toward the creek as if she meant to cry out. Holifield stepped forward quickly and gripped her by the arm. "Don't yell," he snapped. "You want him inside to know?"

The warning silenced her. Flustered and dismayed at being caught, she was slow to find words for her confusion. "You've been here all along!"

The marshal chuckled. "Wouldn't want to miss so touching a scene. It's just too bad Mr. McAlister had to miss it."

"How . . . how did you know?"

"I set it up for you," the lawman said with satisfaction. "Why else do you think I'd put that key on a peg, instead of in my pocket? It wasn't hard to figger you'd snap up the bait, the way you was moon-eyin' that killer tonight. You was around him at supper like a moth around a candle, Mrs. McAlister. You have a soft heart for varmints."

"Why?" she cried in despair. "Why would you do such a thing?" But even as she spoke she knew the answer. "You mean to kill him!"

"He's a dead man already, Mrs. McAlister, thanks be to you. I'll take care of the formalities."

"But he's unarmed!"

"I don't rightly see how me and the deputy can take that chance." Holifield was amused, chuckling as she fell back in revulsion. "Don't you worry about your mare none. I'll see she gets back to you. You'd of done better to turn your outlaw loose on his own horse."

She looked toward the corral. "Mr. Armstrong's there," she said bitterly.

"Uh huh. Well, now, he must be sleepin' sound. But he couldn't have figgered you'd work up such a good case of the sympathies that you'd spring Blaine loose. I reckon I'm just a more suspicious man than the deputy. Anyways, I expect it's no harm done. Blaine won't travel so fast on that little mare that we can't catch him before he gets to his robbers' roost."

"You . . . you're no better than a murderer!" She wouldn't have believed that she could feel such loathing for any man. "That's what you are . . . a killer!"

"I'm the law," J. P. Holifield said angrily. "I'm doin' my duty, is all. I could arrest you for what you've done this night, and don't you forget it. Now you'd best get inside where you belong, and be glad I'm not what you think!"

"I'll tell Mr. McAlister."

The marshal stepped close enough for her to feel his breath warm against her cheek. "I reckon not," he said. "He thinks you're some kind of an angel, a good woman, too good for the likes of him. He might feel different if he was to know about you and Blaine, or how you made calf eyes at that kid that was through here a while back. Might be he'd start to wonder some about you and his hands, too, if he was to learn they been doin' your bidding behind his back, like was done here tonight."

Iris McAlister sagged, the fight knocked out of her. She knew how the marshal could make it all sound, and she couldn't let that happen.

"Good night, Mrs. McAlister," Holifield said.

Despairing, she entered the darkness of the house, and closed the door behind her. She leaned against it, lacking the strength to move. Then she felt the padlock key still gripped in her hand, burning as if it were hot. She thrust it onto the peg beside the door as she had intended. But what good was it now to sneak the key back to its place?

In the silence the clock on the mantel over the fireplace ticked loudly. She thought of Mr. McAlister standing by the mantel at the same hour each evening before he came to bed, winding the clock with exactly the same number of turns, out of old habit. Somehow this small memory, rather than anything else that had happened this night, triggered the flow of tears.

The sorrel-colored mare, tethered to a branch of one of the twin cottonwoods that stood sentinel over the bank of the stream, nickered softly as Blaine approached. She hadn't liked being tied there alone, a fact that suggested a companionable horse, easy to handle. She was scarcely fifteen hands high, nowhere near Randy's size, and Blaine wondered if she was Iris McAlister's own. He had no complaint about size as long as she was willing. If there was anything a cowman hated it was to be afoot, and for a man on the run in this big country to be cut off from his horse was disaster.

He clucked at the mare, tightened the cinch, which had been left loose, and adjusted the stirrups for his long legs. Then he led the horse on foot along the creek bottom. Only when he was a good quarter-mile east of the dark cluster of ranch buildings did he step into the saddle.

It was then he discovered the Colt in a saddle holster tucked next to the horn. It was an oversized Walker, a .44 caliber miniature cannon that Blaine judged to be almost as old as he was. It had a long nine-inch barrel and it must have weighed at least five pounds, accounting for the saddle holster. The thing was just too clumsy and heavy to carry comfortably on a belt or tucked into a waistband. In its long life it had seen a lot of use, including occasional service for pounding nails. At some time it had been converted to accept metallic, rim-fire cartridges, with a rod ejector mounted on the right side of the barrel for ejecting spent casings. There were five of the rim-fire cartridges in the cylinder, the hammer resting on an empty. A hasty search revealed that there was no other ammunition stored on the mare.

A horse and a gun. Blaine was piling up a considerable load of gratitude. To Iris McAlister for helping him escape, and to the unknown cowpoke who had thoughtfully given up a trusty and dependable old revolver to a stranger.

He wondered which of McAlister's hands it had been. The big man they called Brazos Bill? Skinner, the foreman? He shrugged. Probably he would never learn. He had once pegged the group as peace-loving hands who didn't tend to interfere in anyone else's fight, who liked an easy berth and as little trouble as possible. He had short-measured at least one of them. Someone had a sense of fair play and perhaps a dislike of Marshal Holifield. Maybe he had seen too many of the lawman's victims brought back, or had his own feathers ruffled on some occasion by Holifield's arrogance.

In any event Blaine was grateful to him. He would have liked some spare cartridges, just as he would have preferred to be riding his own horse and carrying a rifle or six-shooter more familiar to him, but a man in his situation could be thankful for what he had been given so unexpectedly.

One thing about the big Walker Colt. Blaine had known men to prize such weapons for their size. They were sighted for close-range shooting, but that long barrel would send a ball out as far as a small rifle. It was no match for a rifle's accuracy at two or three hundred yards, but it might surprise someone who thought he was safely out of range.

After her wait the mare was eager to run, and Blaine let her. He didn't slow her down until they were more than a mile down the valley, still heading east. Then he slowed to a walk, stopping occasionally to listen to the night's sounds and to scout his back trail. After a half hour he was convinced that no one followed him.

By then a good many things were puzzling him.

Iris McAlister's actions had been surprising enough. Blaine had given up trying to figure out exactly why she had taken such a risk for a man she knew nothing about, a man who was labeled an outlaw. In the end he settled for the probability that, like the unidentified owner of the Walker, she was getting back at J. P. Holifield. She had made her hatred of the marshal plain enough. It did not even occur to Blaine that there was something in *him* that could touch a woman like her so deeply, awakening a response that would cause her to do something she would normally not dream of.

Analyzing his luck, he began now to doubt it. Not that he had any doubts about Iris McAlister; she had acted honestly, he would swear to that. But it had all been too easy. What didn't ring true was J. P. Holifield's carelessness.

He had left that padlock key where she could find it. Why? Why wouldn't a suspicious man—and the marshal was certainly that—pocket the key? Why post his deputy down by the corral when it would have been just as easy for Armstrong to keep watch over the prisoner himself?

The more he worried these questions, the more dubious Blaine began to feel about his luck.

Finally he pulled up and sat looking back, turned about in the saddle. J. P. Holifield impressed him as being about as straight as a corkscrew. Why would a tricky man risk having his prisoner cut loose?

The answer jumped up clearly. Holifield wanted it this way. He had planned for Blaine to run. It gave him an excuse to track Blaine down, and to kill him.

There was a strong probability that he expected Blaine to be unarmed. If he'd been watching, he would know that Iris McAlister had not given him any weapon.

It would be like shooting rabbits. Holifield would like that. The marshal had more of a sense of humor, plainly, than Blaine had given him credit for, even if it was a cold-blooded man's kind of amusement.

Blaine felt new anger rise. He couldn't help recalling the long day's brooding that had preceded his second encounter with the marshal. There was a price on J. P. Holifield's head, though he didn't know it: in return for him Blaine would get Lem Seevers. Yet he had held back, convinced that there was a line he couldn't cross over, the line between just punishment—call it vengeance, if you wanted to—and murder. Holifield had not been his enemy. He couldn't gun him down in cold blood. There were things a man didn't do, couldn't do if he was to remain the same kind of man.

Holifield was deliberately pushing him over that line. Blaine knew what it meant. Once he crossed over he would be branded an outlaw. He would become a man who would forever after be looking over his shoulder.

There was one other way still open to him. Holifield as yet had no real cause to bring him in. Perhaps that was why he had staged this escape, for didn't it argue that Blaine was guilty if he was afraid to face an inquiry? All Blaine had to do was avoid the marshal until he could prove his case.

All he had to do was run. Dust out. Put mountains and long plains between himself and this overly zealous lawman.

It wasn't hard to find good, sensible arguments for such a course. Lem Seevers had been run down once, he could be found again, perhaps in the open without fifty of Sam Price's men to back him up. And in the meanwhile there were others to find. Tinker Wright. The Clancy brothers and Wes Hannifin, who might not stay penned up for long. Perhaps even others whose names Blaine had not yet learned. Why play into J. P. Holifield's hand when he had doctored the cards?

But all these reasonable arguments were useless. Cullom Blaine wouldn't run. All his life he had been a man willing to skirt trouble, providing that such a detour wasn't too much trouble in itself. He had never sought it out. There was a confidence in him that made it unnecessary for him to prove his courage, either to himself or to others. No man could push him, but he wouldn't force a clash when it made little sense.

The past year had changed him. He was harder now, more stubborn. He had things to do and nothing would stand in his way. Maybe that was what had made many a man an outlaw, the refusal to bend at all.

J. P. Holifield had dealt himself into the game, and he had

used a cold deck. That took it out of Blaine's hands. The choice had been made for him, and he wouldn't run from the consequences.

Cold-eyed, Cullom Blaine turned the mare's head from the east and pointed her south across the valley. That was where Holifield would expect him to go, almost certainly. He'd guess that Blaine would run for cover at Price's Landing, and he would try to cut him off.

But there was a chance that the marshal would wait for first light to "discover" that his prisoner was missing. That would make it look right afterward. The marshal would have McAlister and all his crew as witnesses that his prisoner had shown his brand by running. Then he and his deputy would ride hell-for-leather along Blaine's tracks.

So be it. They would find him waiting for them, and there would be no rules now, no gentleman's code of fighting. Holifield and his deputy stood warned, just as Blaine did.

J. P. Holifield had called the play. Blaine wouldn't disappoint him.

# FOURTEEN

J. P. Holifield's shout brought a couple of McAlister's hands stumbling out of the bunkhouse, one of them without his pants. They saw the marshal running across the yard. About the same time McAlister appeared on the porch behind him, white hair tousled, awkwardly buttoning his shirt and stuffing it into his waistband with his crooked arm while he carried his boots in the other hand.

The marshal shouted again over his shoulder, and this time his words were clearly heard. "Prisoner's escaped!"

That drew everyone's attention to the open padlock and empty chain coiled beside the well.

McAlister's long jaw dropped even further. He stepped forward to the edge of the porch, his boots forgotten in his hand, and gaped toward the well. "How the hell did he manage that?"

"I guessed he was a slippery one," Holifield said. There was exasperation in his tone, although he didn't sound as angry as might have been expected.

He knelt beside the well. When he rose he was holding the rusty lock, staring at it.

"But that lock's open!" McAlister exclaimed.

"Wide as a gate," Holifield called back to him dryly.

"How could he—?" The white-haired rancher looked startled as a thought crowded through his surprise. In two long strides he was back inside the house. He emerged more slowly, a perplexed frown on his face. "The key's still there."

J. P. Holifield raised an eyebrow, as if this news was a surprise to him as well. "It's an old lock," he said. "Might be it didn't close properly. I'd've sworn I heard it click shut myself, and the fault's mine if it didn't."

He left the puzzle there. He knew that it would return later to puzzle McAlister, that he wouldn't be able to stop probing the mystery. That knowledge caused the marshal to indulge in one of his mirthless smiles.

In spite of all the hue and cry outside, Iris McAlister had not put in an appearance. She would take advantage of a woman's modesty, Holifield judged shrewdly, and not appear until she was properly dressed after this sudden awakening in the cool gray just before sunup. By that time she would hope to find him gone.

He had given that little woman a busy night, Holifield thought with a soft chuckle. And probably a sleepless one. He wondered how long she had been lying wide-eyed, waiting for his alarm to sound, worrying over the new threat Holifield now posed to her, the hold his knowledge gave him. That was something to which he would have to give some consideration. Truth was, Iris McAlister was as pretty a woman as a man was likely ever to see in this land of blisters and blizzards. If such a woman was to be reminded that she was indebted to him for her good name . . .

Returning to the house he handed the padlock to McAlister, who turned it over in his hand to examine it. The tall man snapped the lock shut, then tried to open it by hand. It held firm. "Not broken," he muttered. "Hell, he couldn't pick it with his teeth."

"No use frettin' about it," Holifield said. "Never mind, we'll catch him. Leastwise, now we know his story was a lie. I never doubted it anyways, but an innocent man had no need to run. I'd best get after him."

McAlister looked up. For the first time he remembered Armstrong, and his glance shot toward the corral. "Where's your deputy? I thought he was watching Blaine."

"He was at the corral, and I expect he nodded. I sent him off straightaway," Holifield added briskly, forestalling any more questions. "My guess is Blaine will try to hole up with Sam Price's gang if he can. Armstrong is riding to head him off."

No one questioned him, although several of the cowhands from the bunkhouse were now within earshot, drawn by the early morning excitement. No one had heard the deputy ride out, but the fact was something they would discuss later among themselves, not with Holifield.

The truth was that the marshal had sent his young deputy south much earlier in the night, a good hour before Iris McAlister appeared on her errand of mercy for Blaine, a precaution that the marshal had not revealed to her. Holifield had had several reasons for the move. Paramount, of course, was the need to make certain that Blaine would not get clean away. But there had also been the necessity to leave Armstrong out of his detailed plans for the prisoner.

The deputy was eager and enthusiastic, but green. He liked wearing a badge, he liked the extra push it gave him, and he didn't blink over shooting a dangerous runaway. It didn't take many lawmen long to learn to justify such actions. In country as big as this part of West Texas, filled with dangerous and quick-tempered men, and with the law spread as thin as it was, a great many law-abiding men figured that a quick rope or a quicker bullet was the best discouragement there was to lawlessness. The situation involving Blaine was, however, ticklish. Holifield was not certain that he was a wanted man, although he had implied as much to Armstrong. On his own Blaine might not have made a move, and the marshal had had to contrive a way to encourage him. He had chosen to leave Armstrong out of that part of his plans, especially the role Iris McAlister was to play. It would have raised questions in the young deputy's mind, and he would have been unable to keep from talking. Armstrong was too damned eager to talk about his exploits, and J. P. Holifield didn't need that kind of speculation going on behind his back. He was doing what had to be done, and he couldn't be worrying always about dirtying his boots in the process.

So he had told Armstrong only that he was going to give the prisoner a chance to show his true colors. He was going to allow him to ride back to town under his own volition, rather than under guard. If Blaine allowed himself to be taken in that way by Holifield, he would have a chance to prove himself innocent of any wrongdoing. But if he ran for cover, his guilt would be plain. Armstrong wasn't quick enough in his head to question that line of reasoning.

Accordingly, Holifield had sent the deputy back to his regular lookout duty along the trail that led toward Price's Landing. Armstrong was to set up in the hills south of the valley, where he could watch his back trail as well as the route to the south. If Blaine appeared, that meant he was running. The deputy's job then was to pin Blaine down until the marshal arrived to give him help.

There was some risk here, of course, but Armstrong, for all his limitations, had keen eyes and deadly accuracy with his Winchester. Both were a source of great pride to him, and they were the reasons Holifield had taken him on. Holifield knew there was a strong possibility that, by the time he caught up, the man called Blaine would already be climbing the Golden Steps, going to meet his judgment. Unarmed, he stood little chance against a man waiting for him with a rifle and good cover.

Yet there was something different about Blaine, a hard-eyed toughness. Holifield wasn't taking anything for granted, and now he felt the need to pick up the fugitive's tracks without further delay.

"His buckskin's still in the pen," McAlister's foreman,

Skinner, reported after a quick check of the corral and the pasture behind it. "Maybe he's afoot."

There was a cool reserve in Skinner's tone that caused the marshal to study him sharply. Was he the one who had agreed to help Iris McAlister free the outlaw? That was something the marshal intended to find out later, when he had time.

"Is any other horse missing? It'd be a fool that'd try to escape on foot from this valley, and Blaine don't strike me as bein' a fool."

"That sorrel of Mrs. McAlister's was out in the pasture," another man said. "I don't see her, but she kinda likes to wander."

McAlister swore. "Damn him! So he's a horse thief as well! Hell, I'd have sworn you were wrong about Blaine, Marshal, but you had him pegged."

"He left his own horse," Skinner pointed out mildly. "It ain't exactly the same as stealin'."

The comment was sufficient to confirm J. P. Holifield's suspicion of the foreman, but he checkreined his quick anger. He would remember it. From now on Skinner would find this territory an uncomfortable place to hang his hat.

"I'll be riding," the marshal said curtly. "You'll thank Mrs. McAlister for her hospitality for me. I'll see she gets her mare back."

"You'll want some breakfast, Marshal. Coffee, anyways."

"If that renegade can ride with his belly sucked in, so can I."

With that Holifield started toward the corral, a small, bristling man who seemed to get bigger as he stalked away.

He was remembering the relentless purpose he had sensed in Blaine, and he knew he had waited long enough.

When Asa McAlister, troubled, turned away from the dwindling plume of dust that marked the marshal's trail across the valley toward the southern flank of hills, he found his young wife waiting for him inside the door. She was dressed, although her hair had been tied up quickly in a bun and caught in a net. The smell of coffee was a welcome temptation drawing him toward the pot on the kitchen stove. He smiled at Iris, at first not noticing her pale, drawn expression. As always he saw only the fresh, clean loveliness of her.

On the way to the kitchen he paused, his glance straying back to the peg on the wall beside the front door, where the big padlock key was hanging. He frowned. "It don't make any kind of sense," he grumbled. "How'd that fellow open that lock without a key?"

"He didn't," Iris McAlister said.

The rancher, who felt his years at this hour of the morning on the best of days, before he had had his coffee, was slow to catch her meaning. "What's that?"

"I turned him loose," she answered quietly.

Now his gaze was long and searching. "I don't understand."

"That man is no outlaw," she said. "You know that as well as I do, Mr. McAlister. He sat at our table and ate with us."

"You can't judge a man from that," he said. She couldn't remember when he had ever spoken to her so angrily. "You had no right to interfere with the law!"

"The law!" she cried scornfully. "You know what I think of Mr. Holifield and his law. You think the same, if you'd admit it."

"Well, it don't matter what I think. Damn it, woman, that's not for you to decide—neither what I think nor what is the law's business." He caught himself, seeing her flinch from his harsh tone. Then, heavily, he said, "This could mean trouble for us."

"I don't care about that," she said softly. "But I do care what you think. That's why I . . . I had to speak up."

Her heart was pounding with fear. She wanted to tell him everything—that Marshal Holifield knew all about her action, that he had indeed schemed to trick her into it. But she was afraid. After all the thinking she had done during this sleepless night, she no longer believed that J. P. Holifield would reveal more than she had already admitted. He couldn't do so without at the same time revealing that he had *allowed* the prisoner to escape and lied about it. But in telling even part of the truth she believed that she had risked everything, including the worshipful respect this man had given her in place of love. It was as far as she dared to go.

"I'm sorry, Mr. McAlister. I couldn't see him die . . . I couldn't forget those others. You've known how I felt!"

Asa McAlister, who felt older than ever at that moment, also felt his anger slide away. He gazed at his young wife with quick sympathy. The aching wonder that she could be his, a wonder renewed every day of his life, returned now. She was tenderhearted, that was all, a good woman who couldn't bear to see any living thing hurt or abused, much less a man. How could he blame her?

"You've done Blaine no favor," he said gently. "You'd have served him better if you'd let well enough alone, my dear. The marshal will only do what you're afraid of now."

White-faced, she stared up at him, stunned by his quick forgiveness but alarmed by his words. "He'll get away," she whispered.

McAlister shook his head. "You don't know J. P. Holifield. You think you know him, but you don't. I'm sure you did what you thought was right, but when you opened that lock you sent that man to his death."

She burst into tears, pent-up anxiety and fear at last finding release. The tall rancher folded her into his arms, his own eyes filling, and patted her awkwardly, comforting her as a man comforted a child.

# FIFTEEN

The land rose in irregular folds to the base of a low, broken sandstone ridge. Beyond this line of red rock was the long slope that climbed fairly steeply to the foot of the granite hills. It was here, much higher in the hills, that Blaine had been trapped in the scorched meadow less than twenty-four hours ago.

He came to the broken line of sandstone while it was still dark. He had proceeded slowly for the last hour, pausing frequently, and was certain that he was not yet being followed. Yet his hunch about his easy escape had grown stronger. He was convinced that J. P. Holifield had had an unseen hand in it.

He ground-reined the borrowed mare in the shelter of one of the rock piles while he climbed onto the ridge. There he lay in a shadowed crease until first light began to shred the gray curtain that obscured the valley to the north. He studied the pockets of shadow in the rocks around him for any movement. He surveyed the rising slope behind him without finding anything amiss. Always his gaze returned to scan the dim reaches of Asa McAlister's valley.

He saw the lone rider emerging from ground mist while he was still a tiny speck, his movement more guessed at than seen. He wished that he had a pair of field glasses, but the wish was no more than a passing thought. He didn't really need to identify the approaching rider. It was J. P. Holifield.

Was the marshal coming after him alone? What about Armstrong? Did Holifield think that he didn't need help to bring in one man, supposedly unarmed? Or had he chosen, for motives of his own, to make their quarrel personal, *mano a mano?*

Blaine wasn't certain that he knew the lawman well enough to judge. He was cocky. Fearless, or he wouldn't have worn his badge long enough to lose its first shine. But reckless? It didn't seem likely.

More thoughtful now, Blaine climbed down and scooped up the mare's reins. He could wait here for the lawman to come. These red rocks offered some shelter. But with his ancient six-shooter and only five cartridges he would be vulnerable to a determined man, which Holifield certainly was, armed with a rifle and plenty of ammunition. He discarded the notion, not from any moral scruples—the marshal was forewarned now—but because he doubted that the feisty little lawman would blunder carelessly into an ambush.

No, he would make his stand at a place of his own choosing, where he could somehow equalize the disparity in weapons and avoid being bottled up.

Working his way upward through the tumbled sandstone piles, Blaine kept rock between himself and the distant rider until he reached the broad slope that formed an apron for the higher bluffs ahead. Then he rode straight for the hills, avoiding a run that would raise too much dust, his eyes narrowed in speculation as he studied the terrain.

The rise was shot with washes and deeper arroyos cut by runoff from the hills. In the early light these were pools of shadow. Working east of the beaten trail, Blaine had to cross or thread his way among these cuts, none of which held water at this lag end of summer. As he approached the granite bluffs he found his way blocked by an arroyo twenty feet across and ten feet deep. Not liking the look of the crumbling sides of this dry, Blaine rode along the embankment, searching for an easy way into it or some other access to the hills that would avoid a crossing.

Some soft sand at the edge of the embankment suddenly gave way. The mare stumbled. Blaine pitched to the side, struggling for control of the startled horse. At the same moment he heard the crack of a rifle shot.

Blaine swore. He knew instantly that he had underrated the marshal again, that he had been herded like a brainless calf into another trap. Holifield was behind him. Someone else—it had to be the deputy—had been waiting in the hills with a rifle.

But Armstrong, Iris McAlister had said, was guarding the corral, his presence there the reason Blaine had not been able to escape on his own horse. That, too, had been a ruse.

Blaine didn't believe for a moment that the earnest young woman had lied. She had been deceived, and Holifield had been smart enough to know that Blaine would trust her.

With the strength of his hands and arms he kept the mare from skidding into the arroyo, but those few seconds while horse and rider struggled for balance were too long. They were exposed at the top of the embankment, an easy target. Blaine heard the thud of the second bullet striking solid flesh. The distant retort of the rifle was lost in the mare's scream.

She had reared upward into the line of fire, taking the bullet intended for him. They plunged together down the soft bank into the arroyo.

Blaine kicked one boot loose as he fell. The mare toppled over. She landed on her haunches and slid the last few feet to the bottom. Struggling to rise, she screamed again as one foreleg crumpled.

Rage at his own stupidity shook Blaine as he tried to free himself. The blood pounded in his head. Pain lanced his right leg. It was pinned under the kicking horse, exposing him to her thrashing hoofs.

In her frantic struggles the mare rolled away from him. Blaine scrambled clear.

The horse's cries of agony and fear seemed to strike through him, chilling knives of sound. In the gray light at the bottom of the dry he tried to find the big Colt. It was still in its saddle holster.

On his first try to reach the gun, one of the mare's slashing hoofs grazed his shoulder. He dodged back, his right leg buckling. Shakily he waited, fighting the anger that could all too easily stampede him. Then he saw an opening and dove in under the mare's legs. His hand closed on the butt of the Walker. He snaked it from its leather and stumbled back safely.

Blaine knew that there was a good chance that Holifield and Armstrong believed him unarmed, and he hated to give up that edge. What's more, he had only five cartridges in the Colt. Facing a fire fight against two well-armed men, he couldn't spare one of them. Yet he did not hesitate. The mare was his responsibility. He couldn't leave her like that. Only three of her legs were moving. Either the rifle bullet had smashed her shoulder, where she bled profusely, or she had broken a foreleg in her fall.

Blaine stepped in close. He fired one shot, smashing a bullet into her brain.

In the sudden silence he stood trembling. His heart pounded heavily. His right leg, scraped raw in his tumbling fall, throbbed painfully. But he had been lucky enough. His pants leg was ripped open from thigh to ankle. His shoulder and chest ached from other bruises. There was blood on his cheek—his own or the mare's. But as far as he could tell nothing was broken. He was whole, and he was still able to fight.

His fury subsided to a cold anger, which was hardly eased by the reminder that his stupidity had cost the mare her life as well as nearly taking his own.

He couldn't stay where he was. He couldn't let them pin him in this bottom. His one chance was to reach higher ground before they knew exactly where he was, and before there were two guns to catch him in a cross fire.

He had little time. Those rifle shots, which had come from the hills to his right, would have carried far across the valley below. They would certainly have reached the approaching rider, spurring him into a run.

Blaine turned and ran along the arroyo toward the cliffs. He hugged the west wall to avoid showing himself to Armstrong. The dry looped back and forth in a twisting course. Blaine caught a glimpse of bluffs eroded into sharp-edged fissures. Temporary cover there. But would the deputy be able to climb above him, while Holifield closed the door below?

Twenty yards short of the cliffs the arroyo was joined by another, shallower ditch that twisted away to the northeast, cutting diagonally across the long slope until it petered out. Blaine trotted past the fork and stopped short.

He looked back at the wishbone pattern of the two runoffs. While he stood motionless, his mind raced. He was doing exactly what they must have anticipated. Armstrong, who had had a chance to scout the terrain, would have chosen his position well ahead of time. He would certainly have staked out a spot that gave him a commanding view from the heights and was relatively invulnerable as long as he stayed there. There was almost no way Blaine could safely get above him. Blaine was going to be caught in a pincers, and Armstrong was the half he couldn't reach.

But what of Holifield? He had no such advantages. He had no safe niche for himself on the high ground, where he could sit back and wait for Blaine to show himself. The marshal was bringing up the lower jaw of the trap. He had to come up the sloping flats to reach Blaine. And he would have to use the same cover Blaine had—the folds of the land, clusters of rock and brush, washes and deeper cuts in the slope. He was mounted and Blaine was afoot, but he might not yet know that. In any event Holifield would have to dismount to fight effectively in this situation. A man on horseback presented a taller target than a man crawling on his belly.

All this flashed through Cullom Blaine's mind in seconds. He made his decision. The change in tactics meant that he had to confirm young Armstrong's expectations. The deputy would be watching the whole length of the arroyo, trying to catch a glimpse of him. Well, Blaine would have to make it easier for him. . . .

At this point the west bank of the dry was not as high, its lip perhaps eight feet from the bottom. Blaine searched for a foothold. He had lost his hat when the mare pitched into the arroyo. To draw a shot he would have to show Armstrong his head and shoulders.

He was gambling on the fact that no man could hit a small target at long range with a snap shot. Armstrong would have to take aim. And his tendency would be to shoot too quickly when he spotted his target after prolonged delay. By the time the deputy caught Blaine in his sights and squeezed off that first hasty shot, Blaine meant to be down behind the lip.

He didn't think the marshal was close enough yet to draw his fire. That was another chance he had to take.

Blaine found a solid portion of the bank a few feet up. He stepped cautiously onto it. He had the heavy Walker Colt in his hand, hammer thumbed back. With a tight, reckless grin he peered over the rim.

At that moment the rising sun cleared the eastern horizon, bathing the granite cliffs above Blaine's head and their broad flanks in red floods of light. For an instant he was startled by the sudden brilliance. Later he guessed that Armstrong, in his position on the cliffs, must have been blinded momentarily.

Blaine saw the glitter of sunlight on metal, a hundred feet above the slope and perhaps two hundred yards away. He ducked back. A spray of rock and sand bit his cheek. The debris marked the path of a bullet an arm's length to the left of his head. The crack of the shot came almost simultaneously.

Rising quickly, Blaine snapped a shot at the spot on the cliffs where he had caught the gleam of a rifle barrel. In the split second before he dropped back into the hole he saw his bullet bite into rock close by Armstrong's position. Then his boots touched bottom and he ran. At the fork he veered right, racing away from the cliffs along the shallower wash.

His shot had not been intended to hit the deputy, but, astonishingly, the bullet from the remarkable old Colt had carried easily across the two hundred yards, striking just below the shelf at which Blaine had fired. In its long carry it had dropped only a few feet in its trajectory.

That would give Armstrong something to think about, Blaine thought. But his shot had had other purposes. He wanted to make the two lawmen think that, as expected, he was making for the cliffs. And he wanted to convince them that he was armed only with a revolver. The sound of the gunshot should have done that. Like a small dog and a big one, a six gun and a rifle had different barks.

Armstrong might be wondering what kind of handgun could shoot accurately at that distance, but J. P. Holifield would have no such warning. If Blaine's hunch was right, the marshal would be looking for him near the base of the cliffs, and he would be lulled by the belief that he could sit off out of revolver range and pin his target down with rifle fire.

Blaine ran in a low crouch. Before he had gone far the wash widened out, its walls dropping away until they were less than three feet high. He slowed his pace, finally falling into a crab's scuttle. He had covered about fifty yards. He was still well within Armstrong's range, he knew, and he couldn't hope to travel much farther without being spotted by the deputy from his high lookout.

He stopped, dropping onto his belly. Ahead of him the sides of the wash dwindled away. He spotted a cluster of rocks forming a shoulder along the west bank and crawled toward them. There, breathing hard from his run, he stopped again to listen. He'd gone as far as he could safely.

His ragged breathing and heavy heartbeat seemed to drown out all other sound. Where was Holifield now? How close?

Blaine lifted his head cautiously. He was able to keep part of the rock shoulder between himself and the cliffs where Armstrong watched and waited. He found a cleft where two rocks leaned against each other and put one eye to it, peering down the slope.

Across that broad incline between the granite cliffs and the sandstone ridge that marked the bottom of the slope, nothing moved. There were rocks and stunted brush that might have hid a man, but Blaine's sharp gaze found nothing alive. He felt tension crawl along the back of his neck. Holifield could be anywhere by this time. He might have swung to his left, trying to catch Blaine between him and his deputy. That would have put him at Blaine's back.

He turned quickly. To the east the slope was also empty. There was no sign of the marshal.

Bringing his gaze back to the notch that sighted down the slope, he saw a faint haze of dust far down. It was hardly visible at all, no more than the haze a light breeze might stir up. But Blaine felt no breeze at all. The morning was still. In the open it was already warming up rapidly from the direct rays of the sun. The day would be a hot one.

He watched the dust. For a full minute nothing happened. Then a horse and rider eased slowly into view.

In the instant J. P. Holifield appeared to Blaine, he pulled up. He had come around one of the sandstone piles. He carried a rifle in his right hand, the reins in his left. He was leaning forward slightly, peering toward the cliffs along the slash of the arroyo Blaine had followed.

Holifield started forward on his chestnut gelding. He was scanning the ground, and after a moment Blaine guessed that he was looking for an easy way into the arroyo, just as Blaine had done. He was farther away than Armstrong had been when Blaine tried his snap shot, but as the seconds ticked by he edged closer. It took all Blaine's nerve to hold still, refraining from trying an almost impossible shot.

It seemed to Blaine that the marshal's pace would have had a turtle looking back at him, but, step by step, the distance narrowed. Two hundred yards, he guessed. A hundred and ninety. Holifield was watchful all this time, his gaze flicking back and forth between the arroyo below him and the cliffs to the south. He was not yet worried about Blaine and his six gun, but he would take cover soon. Blaine had to act before then.

The moment came abruptly. The marshal found a portion of the arroyo to his liking. He started down the bank. Before Blaine could react, the lawman's chestnut was dropping out of sight, leaving only a pair of haunches and a black tail in view. In a second Holifield would be safe.

Blaine aimed two feet over the marshal's head and fired.

Holifield vanished into the arroyo.

Leaping from his cover, Blaine ran down the slope on an angle that would intersect the arroyo, well below the point where the marshal had disappeared into it. He was moving away from the cliffs and Armstrong's rifle, bobbing and weaving erratically. Even a running target was easy to track along a straight line. Before he had covered half the distance he heard the crack of the deputy's rifle. Blaine didn't know where that bullet went, but a second whined close to his ear and he felt the small hairs rise.

He was a dozen yards from the edge of the dry when the deputy zeroed in with his third shot. Blaine felt something tug at his leg. He stumbled. Off balance, plunging out of control, somehow he stayed on his feet.

Shooting down from the cliffs along a receding slope, Armstrong had placed his first two shots high. On the third he had overcorrected. The low shot struck a loose flap of Blaine's torn pants.

Blaine pitched headlong. Armstrong's fourth shot cut the space where he would have been. Blaine's shoulder hit the top of the embankment. He flopped over and rolled to the bottom in a coil of sand and red dust and gravel.

For a few pounding seconds he lay in his own dust cloud while panic receded. It was no time to rest or congratulate himself on his luck. He didn't know about Holifield.

Had the lawman been hit by that one long shot? Or had he simply dipped out of sight into the dry? If he wasn't crippled, he would be on the move. The pattern of Armstrong's shots and the noise of Blaine's plunge into the gully would have told him where to come.

Scrambling to his feet, Blaine trotted along the bottom of the arroyo toward the cliffs . . . and Holifield.

Cullom Blaine was no six-gun artist. He knew how to shoot accurately, but he had no doubt that J. P. Holifield had buried gunslingers far more skilled than he was. He had to keep their clash from coming down to any such duel of skills. Even if he was unhurt, the marshal would have been shaken up by that surprising revolver shot. His confidence might also have been shaken a little. Blaine wanted to keep after him before he got over his surprise and the uncertainty it might have raised in his mind about his enemy.

The arroyo zigzagged several times between the point of Blaine's plunge and the place where Holifield had disappeared. Blaine ran past the first turn and slowed his pace. He eased around another corner.

He faced a stretch of open bottom. Ten feet wide, the channel was about twenty yards long in a straight line before the wriggling course of the dry took another turn. Without any solid evidence to go on, Blaine knew that J. P. Holifield was around that bend, waiting. The hunch was so strong that he didn't question it.

But it surprised him. He hadn't thought the tough little lawman was the kind to make another man come to him, any more than Blaine was when his blood was up.

Did that mean he was hurt? If so, how badly?

Blaine could hear nothing. Holifield might have chosen to ride along the dry toward the cliffs, of course, refusing to allow Blaine to pick the time and place for their show-down. But Blaine's strong hunch persisted. He could *feel* the marshal's presence around that next turn, so close that each man breathed shallowly rather than give himself away.

Blaine edged along the straight toward the bend. Halfway along he stopped. He had heard something. It might have been a groan or a sigh. Or had he imagined it? The sound—if it had been real at all—was not repeated.

The tension pulled every nerve and muscle in his body tight. A very real fear pounded in his head and in his chest. A man stepping out to face a bullet at close range was a damned fool if he felt no fear. It was not the kind of panic that caused a coward to show his yellow; it was the kind of awareness that made another kind of man brace himself, revealing the solid bone in his spine.

If Holifield was waiting there around the corner as Blaine guessed, he would fire at the first blur of movement. This was no time to ease cautiously into view.

Gathering himself, Cullom Blaine sucked in a breath and charged. He bolted past the turn and threw himself across the floor of the arroyo toward the opposite bank.

The roar of a Winchester filled the canyon. Blaine saw the slash of flame. At the same instant he saw the marshal huddled low against the bank thirty feet away. Blaine skidded hard against the embankment, twisted and fired. He heard the lawman scream.

As quickly as that the fight was over. It took longer seconds for Blaine to sort out the pieces of that sudden violence.

Blaine's gambling shot with the long-barreled Walker Colt had struck Holifield in the back of his right shoulder as he was dropping into the arroyo. The lead ball must have spilled him from his horse, which was nowhere in sight. He had rolled in a lot of dust. The big .44 caliber bullet had torn up the shoulder pretty badly. The lawman's sleeve and shoulder and upper chest were soaked in blood. There was no way of knowing immediately whether the lead had smashed bone or gouged a big hole.

Still conscious, but unable to use his right arm, the marshal had waited for Blaine to come to him. He had been lying on his left side, twisted around enough so that he could hold his rifle balanced across his thigh, his left hand ready to squeeze the trigger. It had been an awkward way for a right-handed man to shoot, worse for a man in pain. Holifield had fired when Blaine charged past the bend. Shooting at the first sign of movement, he had nibbled a piece out of the canyon wall at the turning. The missing chunk was chest-high for a man Blaine's size.

Holifield had been bracing himself with his right hand in spite of the pain in his shoulder. Blaine's hasty shot had smashed that hand or wrist. Pure chance, Blaine thought, as his breathing slowed toward normal, like a locomotive chugging into a station. He had aimed higher and to the right.

The lawman seemed to have slipped into unconsciousness. He lay in a formless, crumpled heap. The blood so bright on his shoulder and right hand might have drained from his face, which was a pasty white. His left hand clutched his chest.

But he was alive, Blaine saw as he approached. His chest was moving.

Blaine went down on one knee beside the marshal. He held his Colt ready, but he didn't think there was any fight left in the lawman, who looked even smaller now. Blaine reached to peel back Holifield's blood-soaked black coat to inspect his shoulder wound. In that moment the marshal made his last move.

His left hand had slipped under his shirt near his waistband. He tried to drag a little hideout gun clear. The stud trigger of the derringer snagged on his shirt.

Cullom Blaine laid the nine-inch barrel of the Walker across Holifield's skull, none too gently. It raised an instant welt, from which blood oozed where the skin was broken. The marshal sagged, out cold.

He was a tough little son of a bitch, Blaine thought grudgingly.

He removed the derringer from Holifield's hand and stuffed it under his own shirt. Then he picked up the marshal's Winchester and slid his six gun from its holster. Stepping back, Blaine felt the first wash of relief since the shooting had started. He had been down to his last cartridge in the borrowed Walker Colt.

His glance went to Holifield's right hand. If the lawman lived, it would be a long time before he used that hand to draw a bead on another outlaw. It wasn't what Blaine had planned, or what Sam Price had had in mind when he proposed his bargain, but J. P. Holifield was no longer a threat to the men of Price's Landing.

The fact gave Blaine no real satisfaction, but it made him think again of Lem Seevers.

The drumming of hoofs jerked Blaine to attention. There was nothing he could do for the marshal immediately, and he wasn't out of this scrape himself. But the hoofbeats surprised him. He guessed at once that the rider was Armstrong. It was just as clear that the deputy had become overanxious about all the shooting. He would have been safer—and more dangerous—if he had stayed up there in the cliffs.

The running steps of the horse died out all of a sudden. Listening hard, Blaine guessed that Armstrong had dived for cover out there on the slope some distance from the arroyo, roughly opposite the place where the marshal had vanished from sight—and where Blaine now stood.

Blaine turned south and trotted along the draw, heading back toward the cliffs. When he had covered some thirty yards he found a notch in the west bank that enabled him to climb easily. He lifted his eyes to the rim and peered over.

In a few seconds he had spotted the young deputy's cover. Even if he hadn't seen the top of Armstrong's hat, he would have placed him quickly, for the deputy called out in a moment of rashness.

"Marshal? You okay?"

Silence answered him. Blaine studied the patch of brush and rocks where the peak of the hat showed. Beyond it the deputy's riderless horse drifted into view, wandering slowly down the slope, then pausing to look back.

"Holifield?" Now the deputy's voice was anxious, sharp-edged by fear.

Armstrong was young, and the same impatience and curiosity that had driven him from his safe perch in the cliffs would eventually drive him out of his present shelter, Blaine thought. He settled where he was, leaning a shoulder against the slant of the embankment.

He didn't have long to wait. Within ten minutes he saw Armstrong slide away from his cover. Blaine brought the marshal's Winchester close to the lip of the bank. But at that moment the deputy dropped to the ground, and a little fold in the terrain hid him from view.

Armstrong began a slow crawl toward the arroyo. Every once in a while Blaine was able to glimpse a piece of hat brim or a shoulder or the projecting curve of the deputy's buttocks as he wriggled along the ground on his belly.

Well, it cut two ways, Blaine thought. If he couldn't see Armstrong, the deputy would have just as much trouble spotting him, as long as he hugged the ground and the youth didn't raise his head to look around him—as he damned well should have before this.

Blaine slid over the top of the embankment and began to worm his way down the gradual slope. He edged toward his left in order to cut behind the deputy's path.

He was halfway there when Armstrong reached the edge of the arroyo. Blaine heard a strangled cry: "Marshal! Oh, Judas—!" He had a brief flash of the deputy's head and shoulders as he jumped into the dry.

Blaine came to his feet. In a crouch he ran toward the draw, moving on his toes to make as little noise as possible. As he closed the gap he could hear Armstrong's choked cries. "Damn you, Blaine, you'll hang for this! If he dies, I'll . . . I'll nail your hide, and hang up your rattles!" To Blaine's surprise there were real tears behind the anguished words. He wouldn't have thought J. P. Holifield could inspire so much loyalty.

But Armstrong hadn't learned much about fighting no-good killers, Blaine thought grimly. If he had, he wouldn't have been making so much noise.

Suddenly he heard the boots scrambling along the bottom of the arroyo. They were moving quickly in the direction of the cliffs. Armstrong must have spotted his tracks going that way, Blaine guessed. He waited for the deputy to draw level with him. The steps went by him, slower now, belatedly cautious.

Blaine stood erect and moved quickly to the edge of the dry. Armstrong had his back to him. He was less than fifteen feet away.

"Whoa up there!" Blaine called sharply.

The deputy started to whirl. Blaine put a bullet from the Winchester past his cheek close enough to fan it. Armstrong went rigid.

The slam of the shot echoed off the cliffs in a sudden silence.

"That'll do fine," Blaine said softly. "Drop the rifle. Good. Now turn around so I can see you." When the deputy had obeyed, Blaine told him to unbuckle his gun belt and let it drop. "You can grab for that iron if you want, but I wouldn't advise it. If you even spit sudden, I won't be accountable for what I might do. I'm a mite tired of you two badge-thumpers ridin' my back."

"You'll be accountable!" Armstrong retorted, his face red, but he did as he was told. "You'll stretch a rope, Blaine. If the marshal goes under—"

"He'll live," Blaine said curtly. "Move on along and you can tend to him."

As Blaine pointed the way with the muzzle of the Winchester, Armstrong retreated along the arroyo. Blaine waited until the deputy was a safe distance away. Then he jumped down into the dry and scooped up the dropped rifle and gun belt. He was beginning to get loaded down with iron, Blaine thought with a kind of grim humor.

It was the first easy moment he had had in twenty-four hours.

Armstrong knew of a small spring at the base of the cliffs. Between them he and Blaine carried the marshal to the spring, which was in shade and offered as good a place as any to leave the wounded man. Using the spring water, Armstrong cleaned out the bullet holes as best he could while Blaine watched. Then Blaine found a spare shirt in Holifield's bag and tore it into strips to use as a bandage. Through all this the deputy, subdued, made no attempt to jump him.

When they had done what they could, Blaine stared down at the little lawman. Holifield was carrying no lead, and even the shoulder wound was more bloody than serious as long as it didn't fester, the bullet having missed bone. But Holifield remained unconscious, and Blaine didn't think he was in any condition to ride double with Armstrong across the valley. Such a ride might start the bleeding again and finish Holifield where hot lead had not.

"You'll have to stay with him," Blaine said without apparent sympathy. "I'll send a wagon back from McAlister's."

"You stealin' my horse too?" Armstrong protested.

"I'll leave 'em both with McAlister," Blaine answered.

He planned to ride the marshal's chestnut, using the deputy's horse to pack the rig from Iris McAlister's dead mare.

"You can't leave us out here without a gun!"

"If a snake comes lookin' for you," Blaine said coldly, "you'll just have to stomp him."

"You're a cold-hearted snake yourself."

"I didn't ask you two to bushwhack me," Blaine said, anger rising. "If I was the hard-biting rattler you take me for, you and the marshal would both be belly up right now, and there'd be none to say Cullom Blaine had any hand in it. Buzzards don't talk much. So just be glad you're wrong, Deputy. And when you deliver the marshal safe, don't be in too much of a hurry to come back. I'd hate to think you was followin' me again, y'hear?"

He left in the heat of anger, after retrieving the mare's saddle and his own battered black hat from the arroyo. He had ridden a good mile across the valley before his temper began to cool. By then he knew that the words he had spoken in anger were true. What followed from them was also true: From this day on, because he had left the two lawmen alive, he would ride outside the law. He was no longer only a hunter. Now he would also be the hunted.

# SIXTEEN

From the first hour the day had been hot, and by mid-morning it was a banked oven. Blaine had ridden hard, alternately riding the marshal's gelding and Armstrong's bay. In spite of the anger he felt toward J. P. Holifield, he was not as indifferent to the lawman's fate as he had sounded in talking to the deputy. He had no wish to see Holifield finish his circle, in spite of what he'd done. Blaine's hatred of the men who had murdered Samantha was implacable. He found it easier to dismiss wrongs done to him.

His punishing pace brought him galloping into Asahel McAlister's yard a full two hours before noon. There was no one in sight as he drew near—it was a good day to be in shade somewhere—but by the time he slowed the lathering chestnut he was riding then to a walk as they passed the bunkhouse, he was attracting attention like a carcass drawing flies in the sun. Two of the ranch hands trotted after him from the bunkhouse to the railing next to the water trough. Asa McAlister's long strides brought him from the house in time to meet Blaine at the trough as he pulled up. A patch of light blue cloth appeared in the doorway off the porch.

Blaine squinted down through his coating of red dust at the white-haired cattleman. His green-flecked eyes were like a couple of holes in old red flannel.

"So it's you, Blaine. Damned if I expected to see you here again." McAlister's tone was flat. Blaine wasn't sure if it was hostile or disturbed. Certainly the easy friendliness he had heard before was missing.

"Wasn't sure myself."

The cattleman's gaze narrowed on the dusty horses. "That's the marshal's horse! And Armstrong's."

"Yes." Blaine's glance flicked toward the woman on the porch. He wondered how much McAlister knew of his escape. "That mare I sneaked off with took one of the deputy's bullets and broke her leg. She was a good one, and

I'm sorry. I owe you for her."

McAlister brushed the matter aside impatiently. "Damn it, man, what happened? If you've done the marshal in, it'll play hell."

"He's hurtin' some," Blaine said dryly, "but he'll live to snarl. I told the deputy you'd send a wagon to bring them both in."

"Armstrong? You told Armstrong?"

Blaine answered the implied question. "That deputy's pride has been bruised some, but I reckon he'll get over that, give him time. He's not a bad sort. I can't say the same for your marshal."

"I can't believe it," McAlister said, staring at him.

Blaine swung down from the saddle and stooped over the trough. He doused his face and the back of his neck with water. He came up shaking his head and grinning from the cool sensation. The sun had sucked him dry, and he would have relished a dunking right then, head to toe. He rubbed the chestnut's muzzle with his wet hand. Ordinarily he wasn't a man to water himself ahead of his horse, but both the gelding and the bay were overheated and he had held them back from the trough. Now he permitted the chestnut a small drink. One of the watching cowpokes did the same for Armstrong's horse.

McAlister was still studying Blaine in disbelief, but there was a hint of respect, even admiration in his gaze. He wasn't angry, Blaine thought. His glance swung again toward the house. It found Iris McAlister standing at the front of the porch, shading her eyes with one hand as she watched the men beside the water trough.

Following Blaine's gaze, McAlister said, "Mrs. McAlister told me what she did." Blaine looked at him quickly. "I can't say as I approve, but . . . I can understand it. She's a good-hearted woman, Mr. Blaine, and she doesn't approve of our marshal any more than you do."

Blaine felt renewed admiration for the lovely young woman across the yard. It had taken a special kind of courage to admit what she had done. "She is a fine woman," he said. "I won't forget what she done. But I suspect Holifield knows, and it won't sit well with him now. You'd best remember that, McAlister."

The tall man nodded soberly. "It's you will have to look to your back trail, Blaine. I never heard of Marshal Holifield bein' bested in anything before. You've made a dangerous enemy. I'd say the fact that the marshal and the deputy are alive tells what kind of man you are, but the marshal won't hear that now. J. P. Holifield's a terrier, Blaine. He won't never let go."

"He won't be bitin' anyone for a spell," Blaine answered quietly.

He turned toward the watching cowhands, who had been taking in the news and exchanged murmured comments. Blaine tugged the Walker Colt from his waistband and held it out by the long barrel. "I found this old-timer packed on that mare. It did just fine, or I wouldn't be here. I figger maybe it belongs to one of you."

Skinner was the one who stepped forward to take the six-shooter from him. Blaine thought he saw a glint of pleasure in the grizzled foreman's eyes, and Blaine himself repressed a grin as Skinner muttered, "I must of forgot it. Sure would've hated to lose ol' Betsy."

By that time Blaine was feeling a delayed weariness

from his busy night and busier morning. McAlister saw the lift of his shoulders against the ache behind them and looked at him inquiringly. "You'll be hungry and thirsty," he said. It was both a question and an offer, and it told Blaine where the rancher stood. His hair was white, Blaine thought, but he still had a young man's sand.

"Thanks, but I'll be riding," he said, not without a passing regret. He was bone-tired, for he had caught only a few hours' sleep while he was chained to the well in the early part of the night, and he was hungry as well. But he saw that his staying would involve McAlister and possibly some of his hands in his quarrel with J. P. Holifield. He didn't want that. They had done enough—more than enough. "I come back for my own horse, and my own gear, and to ask you to send a wagon after them two lawmen. I've other business that calls me."

"It must be important," Asa McAlister said.

Blaine met the gaze of the older man's blue eyes. They were curious but not prying. "It is," he said. That was all, and McAlister expected no more.

"Luck to you, then," McAlister said.

He held out his hand. Cullom Blaine was glad to take it.

Five minutes later Blaine rode away from the headquarters of McAlister's ranch on his fresh buckskin. Randy was prancing with an eagerness for the long ride ahead that awakened in Blaine only a dull envy.

He paused on the top of a low rise to look back. Asa McAlister and a couple of his hands were hitching a team to a springer wagon. Someone was tying a couple of spare horses on leads behind the wagon, and throwing a saddle into the back.

The patch of blue cloth was still visible in the shade of the porch. Blaine lifted his hand to his hat brim.

Then he turned his face south once more. He was already calculating that he could reach Price's Landing by sundown of the following day, if he didn't tarry.

He had carried out his part of the bargain. Now Sam Price could meet his pledge.

# SEVENTEEN

Lem Seevers was afraid of heights.

For three days he had flirted with the caves which rose in tiers almost to the top of Big Belly, the name given by long-time residents of Price's Landing to the immense, hollowed-out rock formation that sheltered the ancient Indian dwellings. The ascending levels were joined either by very narrow, steep flights of steps cut into the back wall, or by rickety pole ladders. Since each layer of caves had to be narrower than the one below it, to make room for the shallow ledge that ran in front of the caves at each level, the higher shelves were more crowded, the steps and footpaths smaller and more precarious. There was no room for a slip or a misstep. Moreover, the highest of these crude stone dwellings, unknown centuries old, had crumbled enough to be considered dangerous. No one in Price's Landing lived on the two topmost levels.

Torn by conflicting fears, Seevers finally worked up nerve enough, late in the afternoon of the fourth day after Cullom Blaine left the Landing, to climb all the way to the top. There he stood against the back wall, his heart beating quickly, not from the climb so much as from nervousness.

He looked out beyond the inhabited table far below him, and his hopes sank.

The Big Belly had its curving back to the southwest. It blocked off the setting sun from a portion of the Landing, throwing that long half into early shadow. The view open to the west revealed an endless, barren plain stretching to the horizon. To the north and east, the tops of hills and the hollows of deep canyons were visible, with here or there a hint of green or a high meadow shining like a sheet of gold in the last gleam of sunlight. But what Lem Seevers had hoped to see—the approaches to Price's Landing, even perhaps the entry to the canyon passage—was cut off, invisible from this angle. In any event, the sun was almost down by the time he reached the highest level of caves, and the lower canyons and flats were already murky pools in which the shadows rose like a black flood.

Disappointed, but in no hurry to face the climb down those treacherous steps and shaking ladders, Seevers looked down at the town below.

Resentment soured his expression. One of Sam Price's guards was squinting up at him. They didn't care if he wanted to spend his energy climbing, but he was never out of the sight of at least one of the guards.

Aside from those appointed to watch him, Seevers had been completely ignored for four days. Not just ignored. Conspicuously avoided.

Damn them all! What right did such a band of murderers and robbers have to treat him like poison?

He looked up again. The sunlight was going out like a lowered wick. The vista spread before Seevers was awesome and beautiful, the sky still a clear blue over the changing pinks and purples and grays of the lonely land-scape, but he saw no beauty in it. The vast, empty plains to the northwest receded into a gloom that matched his own brooding mood.

The gathering dusk forced him down, cautiously at first, then more quickly as the crowded ledges widened and the way became easier. He didn't breathe easily until he was back on the broad stone table that held the main buildings of the camp.

Price's Landing came alive at dusk, as if its residents welcomed darkness and a few hours of false gaiety, the bright glow of lanterns illuminating the buildings, the saloon spilling over with boisterous activity. All the men drank more at night. The poker and faro tables were more crowded. The six women in the back rooms of the saloon—four Indians and two Mexicans—were kept busy, lines often forming outside.

Lem Seevers wandered through the camp alone. His guards made no attempt to follow him closely. He was on a long rope as long as he didn't stray near the corral or off in the direction of the canyon exit.

Seevers bumped into a blocky figure. As the man moved away, he recognized Chico. "Hey, Chico! How's about cuttin' some of the dust?"

The Mexican muttered something in Spanish and showed his back. Seevers scowled after him, biting off an angry curse.

Two other men Seevers knew, both Texians, who had been friendly enough before Blaine's coming, gave his invitation cold stares and walked away from him, their steps deliberately unhurried, contemptuous. Moments later

Seevers saw the two enter the saloon together.

He swore aloud.

The story of the woman who had been burned alive had spread quickly through the camp. Now he was being treated like he was dirt, or worse, like he had a high skunk smell that might rub off.

To hell with them! He'd be gone soon enough. Cullom Blaine wouldn't be back, they all knew that. Seevers had been shocked and alarmed by Sam Price's deal with Blaine, but he had later talked the fear away. Or most of it. How could Blaine keep his part of the bargain? He'd have to be crazy to go against a lawman that way. And not just any lawman. J. P. Holifield wasn't just the ordinary fat-bellied town sheriff.

No, Blaine wouldn't be back. He'd pulled a bluff and saved his hide, that was all.

Word would come in another day or two. Or Sam Price would send someone out to see what had happened, if anything. Then Seevers would ride away from the Landing and never look back. He would leave Texas and Blaine and all of it behind him, go south into Mexico or maybe all the way west to California, where he wasn't known. Maybe he'd even get a job and go straight for a while.

Or maybe he wouldn't do anything of the kind, he thought, with a trace of his old arrogance. Hell, even Abe Stillwell had had respect for Lem Seevers' six gun. He'd make some of Sam Price's flannelmouth badmen dance if he ever caught them alone!

It was strange, but none of them, with the possible exception of Price himself, turned Lem Seevers' backbone to jelly in the way Cullom Blaine did.

Seevers had been lurking back in the crowd when Blaine was taken from the tiny jailhouse to the camp's meeting hall. He had seen Blaine's gaze darting over the crowd, searching for him, and when those bright eyes touched him he had ducked back out of sight, unable to check the impulse or to deny the terror that softened his spine.

Hell, it didn't even make sense! Blaine was an ordinary-looking man, no bigger than many of the outlaws of the Landing, with the average number of eyes and ears, arms and legs. Why did sight of him strike fear so deep that Seevers had to fight a lurch of sickness in his belly?

Maybe it wasn't fear at all. Maybe it was only the shame of remembering Blaine's woman.

But Abe Stillwell was dead. Brownie Hayes was gone. The man who had done that was no ordinary man, no matter what he looked like.

Seevers found himself wishing, for perhaps the hundredth time in the past few days, that Blaine *had* ridden away from Price's Landing to challenge J. P. Holifield. That would be something, if a marshal lifted the fear from Seevers' back.

Restless and uneasy, Lem Seevers decided on impulse to seek out Sam Price. At least the outlaw chief would talk to him.

Sam Price lived in the largest of the old cave dwellings at the bottom of the Big Belly. He had his own Mexican woman to cook and care for him. Seevers found him reclining in a string hammock in front of the cave, smoking a black cigar. He had eaten a short time before, and the smoky smell of *carnitas* reminded Seevers that he had had no supper. He hinted as much, but Sam Price ignored the hint.

Still, Price acknowledged his greeting, Seevers thought sourly. He sat on a stone bench, almost grateful for Price's indifferent welcome. Not that he had any real reason to be grateful to the outlaw, although Seevers couldn't believe that Price had meant to keep his announced deal with Blaine. No man on the dodge would ever trust his life to Price's Landing if such a bargain were kept, and Price knew it.

"How long you gonna wait?" Seevers asked suddenly. "About Blaine, I mean."

Sam Price blew cigar smoke skyward. "No hurry," he said.

"No hurry for you! How about me? How long am I supposed to wait?"

"Maybe you should start runnin' now." Sam Price made no attempt to conceal his contempt. "Runnin' seems to be what you're good at."

Seevers flushed. "How am I supposed to do that? You know I can't do that. You put guards to watch me. You said yourself you'd keep me here till Blaine come back, or you heard he was dead or run off."

Price's black eye stared at him. It was disconcerting not to know if the other, hooded eye could also see clearly. "I hear other things," Price murmured.

"What's that?"

"There's some that thinks you give the Landing a bad name. You got more than Blaine to worry about."

"You couldn't let nothin' happen to me!" Seevers cried in momentary panic. "I got as much right here as any man. A man on the dodge is supposed to be safe here. What's Sam

Price's hideout worth if it ain't safe? Nothin'!"

"You got no rights but what I say you have," Price answered coldly. "And you lied to me."

"I din't lie! I was only . . ."

Seevers' protest faltered. Price believed Blaine's story. They all did. It wasn't fair. Seevers hadn't liked killing the woman that way. It hadn't been his idea at all. He had told Blaine so, as he had assured himself a thousand times in the long months since that fiery night, which seemed now a time of madness. The whole bunch had become crazed by anger and greed and lust. Seevers had been carried along with the others, as helpless as a man caught in a flood. Why should he be blamed?

"I don't give a damn what you done to that woman," Price said, as if answering his question. "And there's a score of men here has done worse. But you come runnin' on a lathered horse, claimin' a bounty hunter was on your tail. You lied about that. Wouldn't surprise me if the town decided to string you up to save Blaine the trouble."

"What makes you so goddamn sure Blaine talks straight," Seevers blustered. "You think he'd admit bein' a bounty man?"

"He wouldn't have come. Ain't enough money to make Blaine follow you to Price's Landing just for that. Maybe he's loco, but he spoke straight. He might even be crazy enough to come back."

"You said no man could buck that marshal!"

"I didn't say no man. I said no ordinary man." Price regarded Seevers speculatively, his good eye narrowed. "Would you say this Blaine was an ordinary man?"

Lem Seevers thought of the dogged pursuit that had

hounded him all these weeks out of Fort Worth, tireless, relentless. Sam Price was right. Blaine was some kind of a crazy man. Losing his woman that way had made him crazy. And suddenly Seevers knew that Blaine, somehow, would keep his bargain with Sam Price. Not even that marshal would stop him. It was like he wasn't human.

"You're gonna turn me over to him." Seevers' voice quavered with bitter anger. "You know he'll come back, and you'll sell me out. He offered you money—blood money!"

Sam Price spilled out of his hammock so fast that Seevers didn't know what was happening. He felt his legs kicked out from under him and he was knocked off his bench by a savage backhand blow that cut his mouth. He lit on his back. His head cracked against rock, leaving him dizzy.

Then a big hand caught his shirt at the neck and twisted tight, choking him as he was dragged to his knees. The point of a knife bit into his throat, drawing a tear of blood. In his terror Seevers' hand dropped instinctively toward his six-shooter.

"Touch it and I'll gullet you!"

Seevers froze. He knelt at Sam Price's feet, helpless, convinced that he had bought his last ticket. The belief wasn't strong enough to make him risk going out like a man. His gun hand remained still.

"I . . . I wasn't gonna . . . hell, Sam, you jist took me so quick I was wool-headed. I din't know . . ."

"You knew! You knew what you was reachin' for, just like you knew what you was sayin'. Sam Price don't take blood money for anyone comes to Price's Landing!"

"But . . . you bargained with that Blaine. You promised him!"

Sam Price pushed him away contemptuously. His knife disappeared with a quick move of his hand. Seevers couldn't even see where the blade went. It was quite dark now at the base of the Big Belly, and the cooking fires here and there deepened the shadows away from the light.

"I took a chance Blaine might do somethin' I wanted done," Sam Price said, staring thoughtfully across the shelf at his camp. At the far end of the table a rider was approaching in a hurry. In the failing light it was impossible to see who he was or why he rode at a gallop. "That don't mean I intended to keep the bargain."

Lem Seevers shuddered with relief. The feeling was so intense that it wrung a giggle from him. "Hell, Sam! I should of knowed! I never should of—"

"It won't save your skin!" Price cut him off savagely. "There's others will see you skinned and roasted before you'll ride off this Landing. I can't stop that. I can keep an outsider from gettin' at you or any other man comes here. But I can't follow you around in the dark and keep all the town wolves back."

"My God!"

"Yeah. You'd best do some prayin'. When you're done with that, I'd advise you to do what I said before. Start runnin'."

"How can I? You got me watched. They'd never let me go down canyon, not knowin' about Blaine. You know that."

"There's the back trail. Nobody'd expect you to go that way, so you wouldn't be watched close." Sam Price had lost interest. He was peering across the landing toward the head of the canyon, frowning. Something was happening off there in the gathering dark. He had a hunch, and felt a nudge of surprise.

"That Indian trail?" Seevers whined. "I'd have to go afoot! Even if I could get down thataway, and they say nobody here has ever done it, I'd be on foot with fifty miles of dry to cross. They say that track's half gone. Even if you could do it in daylight, it'd be murder to send me down that trail at night. You might as well hang me up to dry and be done with it."

"It can be walked," Sam Price said curtly. "Once you get out from behind this Big Belly you'll have an hour's light. Ain't sayin' it's easy, but it can be done. But stay or run, I don't give me a damn." Price knew now that his hunch was accurate. There was excitement sweeping through the camp toward him like a dry wind, scattering shouts and calls like leaves before it. "You'd best make up your mind pronto, Seevers, whilst you have the chance. Looks like your man Blaine has come to make his claim!"

# EIGHTEEN

On the way in Cullom Blaine answered Shaughnessy's eager questions briefly. The square-jawed sentry, who seemed to have taken a liking to Blaine, was jubilant. As he and Blaine rode through the camp, he shouted out the sketchy facts he had learned of the shoot-out in response to excited questions. The story flew before the two riders. Excitement mounted, swirling around the procession that became a parade toward the meeting hall.

At the hall Blaine was disarmed and escorted inside. Some of the council members were already there, and the others arrived quickly. What seemed like every man in the camp tried to crowd inside, lining the walls on both sides behind the council tables.

Cullom Blaine sat in the center of the jammed hall as before, facing the horseshoe arrangement of tables and benches. Two hanging kerosene lanterns, suspended from wrought-iron hooks on each of the long side walls, threw a yellow light over the scene, exaggerating the features of the grinning, jostling spectators, leaving deep shadows at the back of the hall.

Sam Price was the last to arrive.

After Price had taken his seat behind his judge's table facing Blaine, he quickly commanded quiet. Blaine then told his story tersely. He recounted his capture by the marshal and his deputy—leaving out the fact that he had intended to ask the lawman for his help. Sketching his escape, he also omitted the role Iris McAlister had played.

"Seems like you got away easy," Sam Price said skeptically.

"I did," Blaine answered. "That's how Holifield wanted it . . . so's he'd have an excuse to use his gun."

There was a murmur of interested reaction. Frowning, Price said, "Go on."

Blaine finished the tale quickly, explaining how Holifield's ambush had been turned against him, and how, in the shoot-out that followed, the marshal had been dropped by two bullets, one of which had smashed his gun hand.

Bedlam filled the meeting hall. It took Sam Price five

minutes to restore order enough to be heard. When he was finally able to speak, his words were blunt. "You sayin' Holifield is still alive?"

"That's the size of it. But he won't be troubling you."

"That ain't the point," Price growled. "Point is, he ain't dead, and that means you din't keep your part of the bargain."

For the second time the meeting hall erupted into an uproar of shouting and general chaos. But there was a difference. This time the hubbub held an angry undercurrent. Instead of cheering and laughing, spectators yelled at each other or threw protests at the outlaw leader.

Price sat calmly behind his table, riding out the storm. Then he pounded his gun butt on the boards. Its banging was lost in the general furor. Blaine saw that Taggart's mourner's face was a dark red with his fury. Blaine frowned. He didn't like the way an open clash was shaping up, pitting rival elements in the camp against each other.

He stared at Sam Price, and it seemed to him that there was a mocking smile lurking behind that one open black eye. All Blaine wanted was what Price had promised, and for the first time he realized that the deal had been a fraud. Price had never meant to keep his part of it. Probably he hadn't expected matters to get this far. Now that they had, he was going to wriggle out of his pledge.

If Price had expected to see quick hot anger in Blaine, he was disappointed. Blaine's face remained impassive, but his stare was fixed and hard—and challenging. Sam Price felt the lash of that challenge as sharply as the cut of a whip.

Blaine spoke. "I kept my part of the bargain. Now

you'll keep yours."

Few could hear him. Blaine wasn't even sure that Sam Price heard, close as he was. But Price caught his meaning if not the words themselves. The mockery in his good eye shaded quickly to a dark malevolence, an answer to Blaine's stubborn demand.

Suddenly Price flipped his gun around and fired a shot into the ceiling. The gun's roar burned through the bedlam in the hall. A sudden hush fell. The bite of powder smoke reached Blaine's nostrils.

"Any more of that," Sam Price said, glaring around the room, "and I'll clear this hall, one way or another."

"You made a deal, Price!" someone yelled from the back of the long, narrow hall, where the light of the two lanterns penetrated only dimly.

"I'll make you another one right now," Price answered. He spoke quietly, but in the silence that now seemed charged, like the still air before a storm, no man failed to hear the threat in Price's tone. "Next man tries to interfere with this council's business better be just the smell of dust before sunup. He'll answer to me personal if he stays."

Here and there in the crowd there was a restless, resentful stirring at the open threat, but there were no more vocal protests. Sam Price was still king of the hill.

When it was evident that he had cowed the crowd, Price brought his baleful stare back to Cullom Blaine. "Council will vote on your claim, Blaine. But I say the bargain was to put Holifield under. You didn't do that, on your own say-so."

"He did as good," Taggart declared. "If Holifield is crippled like he says, then he's off our backs, and that's what we wanted."

"We only got his word for that," Price pointed out.

"That's easy enough," Sims put in. "We could send a man out to prove it, but I'm thinkin' we don't have to. I'll take Blaine's word. Hell, he knows damned well he couldn't get by with lyin' about it."

"You each got one vote," Price retorted.

He sounded confident, and Blaine guessed that he had good reason. He knew his council. Early, the sour-faced bank clerk, was grimacing in his deceptively surly way, but Blaine reckoned that he would vote as he had before, siding with Sims and Taggart against Price. Those three votes would be offset by the remaining three council members. The one called Olsen, a slab-chested gent with wide shoulders and pale, empty eyes, was with Price all the way. There was no sympathy for Blaine in those eyes. The last two men, for whom Shaughnessy had supplied names, were known gunfighters. One, Tidrow, was wanted by Wells Fargo for robbery and the killing of a stage driver and guard. He was a quiet, gray-faced man. Even the hard-cases of Price's Landing stepped softly around him. The other, Rivers, younger and darker, with a badly pock-marked face that looked as if someone had dug bird shot out of it, was wanted in a half-dozen places for murder. He was the more vicious killer, Shaughnessy thought. Tidrow didn't seek trouble; Rivers courted it. The two men had voted with Sam Price before. There was no reason to think they would change allegiance now.

Cullom Blaine stared at Price with cold anger. The bargain was not one he had sought to keep, in plain truth; it had gone against his grain. Only J. P. Holifield's belligerence had brought on the shooting. Nevertheless, the outcome was what Sam Price had asked for. Why was he backing out on his promise? For Lem Seevers? Why should he care about him?

That wasn't the reason, Blaine thought. Sam Price was a complex man. The motives and passions that moved him were not simple and obvious. But almost certainly what it had come down to was Price's ability to rule Price's Landing as he saw fit. He didn't really care about Seevers or Blaine, but he cared deeply about his town and his dominance of it. Because of its reputation as a safe refuge, because he saw open defiance of his power in Taggart's opposition, or because he sensed that Blaine's own challenge could not be ignored, Sam Price had taken a stand. He couldn't budge from it without losing more than he was willing to lose.

"Council can vote," Sam Price said with an air of finality.

"Hell, what's to vote on?" the little bank clerk, Early, said, continuing to surprise. "We made this man a promise. You made it, Price, speaking for the council and every man on this Landing. Blaine did what you asked, when no one thought he could. You said he had to do us a favor, that was the way it was said, if he wanted a favor from us. Well, Blaine did us that favor. If we break our promise now, it means our word isn't worth sand in a twister!"

In spite of Price's warnings there was a muttering of assent and approval when Early sat back. Price's glare shot around the room, then returned to Early. There was more than anger in that black-eyed stare, Blaine saw; there was also surprise. The little bank teller had probably been put on the council because Sam Price had never really intended

176

to give up his right to rule his town, and he had judged that Early would be easily bullied. Politics didn't change, even among thieves, Blaine thought, but sometimes people had more to them than showed on the surface.

"I say the deal was to see Marshal Holifield buck out for good, and that ain't what's happened. Maybe he's hurtin' some, but that don't mean he won't heal good enough to come back and give us the same trouble as before. I'm bettin' he'll be there before first snow, and just as sure." Price paused to let his argument sink in. Then he said evenly, "So I says we vote."

No one dared to push a challenge further, Blaine saw. The voting began. He paid little attention, certain how it would go, just as Sam Price was certain that he had the deciding vote.

But it wouldn't end there. Blaine hadn't ridden so far to be stopped by anyone, even Sam Price.

The voting went as expected, coming down to the last of the council, Tidrow. When the gunfighter failed to speak up as quickly as the others, the murmuring of the spectators in the long hall died away to a hush of expectation. Tidrow did not look at Blaine. His voice was quiet, as colorless as his face, but there was no weakness in it either.

"I never was party to ringin' in a cold deck after the game was started, or any other kind of shade work," Tidrow said. "I don't figger to start now. You don't like the way the cards turned up, Price, you shouldn't have started the game in the first place. I vote we play it the way it was set up. That means the vote's four and two against you, and for this man Blaine. That means we turn that woman-killer over to him, just like it was said when the cards was dealt."

No banging of a gavel could control the crowd's explosive reaction. There were shouts of outrage or support on both sides. One man shoved another and the two had to be pulled apart. The moment held the rumbling threat and movement of a stampede about to break loose. All it needed was a single spark.

Sam Price jumped to his feet. "You'll answer to me, Tidrow!"

But it was Cullom Blaine who rose to face him. "It's me you're double-crossing, Price. You made a slippery bargain. It's me that's holding you to it."

When Sam Price swung toward him, the glitter in his good eye was unmistakable. Behind the hostile anger was something else: satisfaction.

"Then you'll do it my way," Price said. "And my way's with a knife."

Blaine was not surprised. That hooded left eye of Price's had been formed by someone else's blade of steel.

Their clash had come down to what now seemed inevitable, as if it had been so decreed from the moment Blaine rode into Price's Landing. There was no other way, either for Price or Blaine. The Landing was ready to explode in smoky conflict. Caught between two rival factions, unarmed, Blaine would hardly come out of such a bloodletting alive.

The only way he would ever reach Lem Seevers now was to walk over Sam Price's body.

# NINETEEN

"You roped yourself plenty of trouble," Shaughnessy said into Blaine's ear.

"I know that."

It was Shaughnessy who had volunteered his own knife to Blaine. The hall was being cleared at Sam Price's order. The outlaw leader had laid down the rules of the fight: he and Blaine would be locked together in the meeting hall, each armed only with a knife. The man who walked out would have his way.

Shaughnessy, in the few seconds he had before leaving, confirmed Blaine's hunch that it wouldn't work that way. If Blaine survived Price's knife, others would cut him down. The man who killed Price would never live to brag about it. There were too many of Price's followers in the crowd who wouldn't tolerate such a result.

"You got one chance," Shaughnessy said quickly. "If you don't have your heart cut out, that is. You can take the same way Seevers has."

"What do you mean?" Blaine demanded, alerted.

"Way I hear, he lit out when you showed up tonight. He's headin' down that old Indian track. Likely he'll get hisself killed anyways, but I reckon he figgered it was his only way out. You could take the same."

"If someone doesn't gun me down first."

Shaughnessy scowled. "If you're the one opens that door," he said, nodding toward the only entrance into the meeting hall, "maybe I can figger a way. It'll have to be sudden, but I'll be there."

"So will I," Blaine said.

The hall was nearly empty now. Blaine's glance found Sam Price at the far end, standing alone. He was grinning like a man who had had things turn out his way just when they had looked dark. Then something he saw in the bright-flecked eyes of the dusty stranger caused Sam Price's grin to fade.

An expert knife fighter knew he couldn't lose.

There were countless men in the West—tough, stubborn men who wouldn't step aside for a charging bull—who thought twice about going against a blazing six gun at close quarters. The trouble with such a way of settling quarrels, from the average man's point of view, was that, at the eye-ball distances generally favored for such warfare, seldom farther than a dry man could spit with the wind, even a weak-eyed tenderfoot might get lucky enough to hit a man-sized target. And the damage a .44 or .45 caliber slug of lead could inflict upon flesh and bone at such close range was savage. So if a cowpoke preferred an eye-gouging, boot-stomping brawl to a shoot-out, no one called him coward.

And if a man had a special skill with another kind of weapon, a bullwhip, say, or a bowie knife, he'd fight that way every time. An expert with a whip or a knife had little to worry him from an ordinary fighter. He knew exactly how such a duel would come out. He could end it quickly or, if he had a strain of cruelty in him, draw it out. Blaine guessed that Sam Price had that strain. He could whittle away like a wood carver, taking off shavings of hair and skin. It was said that a real champion knifeman could shave

an opponent from hairline to heels without drawing blood
. . . until he was ready to finish off his then hairless foe.

Blaine guessed that Price's skill with a knife probably
had much to do with his long rule over his Landing. Men
who wore their guns low and, unlike the ordinary cowpoker, feared no man's lead, would hesitate over facing
Price's unsheathed steel.

Board shutters had already been secured over the narrow
windows in the east and south walls of the hall, muffling
the sounds of excited talk from outside. When the door
closed behind him, Blaine dropped the bar into place, and
turned.

"Come and get it, Blaine," Sam Price taunted him. "It'll
go harder if I have to come after you."

As if to encourage Blaine he grabbed the long plank table
from which he directed the council meetings and flung it
aside. The table turned over and toppled onto its side. The
other tables and benches were still in position, creating an
aisle between them, restricting Blaine's movement to either
side as he advanced slowly toward Price. Blaine saw this
tactic, and the way the glitter from the lanterns off Price's
long knife was reflected in the shine of his good eye, and
the practiced assurance in the slow dance of the outlaw's
bowie blade, back and forth, tilted upward, ready to strike.

Cullom Blaine had once been known as a patient man
who would ride a long way around to avoid a pointless
fight. At the same time no one had ever mistaken that sensible attitude, because there had been times when avoiding
a wrangle wasn't possible or reasonable. At such times
Blaine had shown himself to be a heller who came into a
fight with every claw extended. Once the battle started,

Blaine never waited for the other man to come to him. He had learned that if you kept after most men, never giving them time to collect their wits or to take your measure accurately, forcing them to react to what you did instead of initiating their own moves, you took away a little of whatever edge they might have.

Sam Price had chosen a knife fight because he believed he could beat any man in such a duel. The instinct that rode Blaine when his blood was up told him that his one chance was to go right after Price and stay on top of him. He knew he would be cut, but he couldn't fight Price *his* way, thrust and parry, letting experience and skill control what happened. He had to carry the fight to Price even if it meant walking right into that ten-inch length of steel. It was the only way Blaine knew how to fight. And it was the one way that might cause Sam Price to lose his nerve.

When he was ten feet from the outlaw, Blaine charged.

The sudden, crude attack surprised Sam Price. No one had ever defied his knife that way. Blaine rushed at an angle, shifting stride as he bulled forward. The movement prevented Price from making a deep thrust. Instead he tried to evade Blaine's assault and to exact a heavy cost. He brought the curving back of the bowie knife down in a chopping backhand stroke. Blaine took the blow on his upraised left arm. Then he bowled into Price at full tilt. The two men went down as if they'd run into a neck-high rope.

Sam Price grunted as his head slammed back against the rock-hard floor. His right hand went slack for a split second, and his knife spilled from his fingers. Before his hand could close again over the hilt Blaine leaped onto him. Price had to grab wildly for Blaine's wrist to keep his knife away. For the first time the outlaw felt his gut cramp in fear.

It wasn't supposed to happen this way—Sam Price had cut up too many men to have anything like this happen to him. But, looking up into Blaine's stony face, into eyes as bleak and pitiless as his own, Price knew that he had underestimated the man.

And Sam Price panicked.

His knife was forgotten. The only thought pounding in his brain was to get this wildcat off his chest and to escape the cutting steel by which he had ruled so long. With all his strength the outlaw kicked and twisted. In his wildness he somehow threw Blaine off.

Price rolled the wrong way—away from the knife he had dropped. When he jumped toward it, Blaine blocked his way. The outlaw retreated hastily, circling behind one of the side tables. As Blaine stalked him, Price picked up the bench behind the table and threw it.

Blaine ducked clear. The long bench, careening upended across the room, caught one of the hanging lanterns and smashed it off its hook. The lamp bounced off the wall, shattering. Cage and glass and kerosene spilled over the falling bench.

Within seconds flames licked upward as the burning kerosene found fresh fuel in the dry planks.

Sam Price saw Blaine jump back from the spill and the sudden, leaping flames, but he failed to see the horror in Blaine's eyes. No one but his friend Tom Wills could have guessed how that dancing fire affected Blaine, how the crackling wood and the hot smoke burned away a protective shell of reason to expose a core of something like madness. If Price had noticed, the fight might have ended differently.

But all the outlaw saw was Blaine's quick dodge—and the way opened to reach his knife on the floor. Blaine had been lucky once, but if Price could retrieve his knife . . .

In one motion he shoved the nearest table toward Blaine and dove across the floor toward his knife. Price landed short, skidded, rolled, and felt his fingers close on the hilt. Exulting, Sam Price twisted around, confidence surging back from the familiar heft of his heavy blade.

He turned straight into the blind, reflex thrust of Cullom Blaine's arm and its extending tongue of steel.

There was a lot of smoke obscuring the room. The table Sam Price had pushed had piled against the burning bench, and it quickly caught fire. There was a din of shouting outside and a heavy pounding against the door, which was barred on the inside.

Cullom Blaine choked back his witless fear of the fire. He didn't even glance at Sam Price, who lay on his back, moaning. The knife blade had gone in under his ribs until Blaine felt his knuckles digging into flesh. He had left the knife there.

As reason returned, Blaine remembered Shaughnessy's warning. He wasn't in the clear. Looking around, his glance fell on another bench. He dragged it across the floor and placed it crosswise where it would just clear the swing of the door when it opened.

Then he went over to the remaining lantern and took it down. He hesitated. In an angry spasm he threw the lantern across the room. It smashed against the already burning bench. New flames spurted across the bench and table.

Standing near the door, Blaine waited for the flames to leap higher, the smoke in the room to thicken. He could feel the hairs crawling up the back of his neck and skull. He fought back a choking cough, held his breath, allowed himself a fleeting hope that Shaughnessy was as good as his word, and threw up the bar.

Under the pressing weight of the men outside, the door exploded open. A mass of bodies spilled into the smoky, darkened room, lit only by the flames. Pushed forward by the pressure behind them, the first men into the room blundered into the low bench in their path and fell over it. Others piled into them. In seconds there was chaos, a tangle of flailing arms and legs, of shouting, cursing men.

In that confusion Cullom Blaine wormed through the edge of the pack and popped into the open like a seed squirting from a melon.

Someone grabbed his arm and jerked him aside. "After me!" Shaughnessy rasped in his ear.

Blaine followed him on the run, stumbling in the darkness before his eyes could adjust to the change. An image of flames continued to dance before his eyes. Once, when he almost fell, Shaughnessy caught him and dragged him forward. Then Blaine was running free, his vision clearing. He tasted the deliciousness of the cool fresh air, sucking it deep into his lungs.

Shaughnessy led him directly to the narrow Indian path that snaked away from the Big Belly behind the main buildings of the camp, vanishing into the hills to the south. When they reached the old track, Shaughnessy stopped. The pandemonium at the meeting hall was far behind them.

"You hurt?" Shaughnessy asked.

Blaine raised his left arm. He'd forgotten his cut. The sleeve of his shirt was blood-soaked.

Shaughnessy tore the sleeve up to the shoulder and examined the cut as well as he could by starlight. "It's deep," he said, "but the blood ain't jumping."

Working quickly, the outlaw ripped his own bandanna into strips. He bound off the wound and bandaged it. When he was finished he peered intently at Blaine. He still found it hard to swallow the fact that this silent man had been locked into a room with Sam Price, and that Blaine had been the one who walked out.

Shaughnessy thrust his own six-shooter into Blaine's hand. "Your man is down there somewhere," he growled. "He's got maybe an hour's start, but . . ." He shook his head. "Hell, I'd hate to be in his boots!"

# TWENTY

As Cullom Blaine started down the path, two shots in quick succession caused him to look back. Shaughnessy had disappeared, but the low buildings of the camp with their few lights were visible below him. Blaine could see the light wavering behind the shutters over one window of the meeting hall, and spilling from the open doorway. Figures still milled around that opening, and there were angry shouts. Another shot crashed. Then silence.

Someone had to take charge soon, he thought, or there would be civil war this night at Price's Landing.

He turned away. As soon as the hump of a steep rise

came between him and the landing, he wiped it from his mind as completely as it had vanished from his sight.

The trail was easy at first, worn smooth, in places a ledge cut into solid rock. It twisted around the south face of a hill, and for a time, being in the open, was clearly lit by the moon and stars, a white ribbon visible for twenty or thirty yards ahead. Then the ribbon followed the contour of the hill to the left, winding between two high precipices into a deep well of darkness.

Blaine moved cautiously along the ledge. He tried to put himself in Seevers' place. Would he keep running? Or would he make a stand? In the other man's boots, Blaine knew, he would have found some good cover that over-looked his back trail and waited. In this situation the hunted man had every advantage. He could set up and wait for the hunter to come, knowing there was only a single narrow track to watch. But did Seevers have enough sand in him for that? Until now he hadn't shown it.

As the trail wound lower between the hills, Blaine was able to see only a few yards ahead, sometimes only a few feet. Then the ribbon cut back sharply and the darkness was almost complete. He had to feel his way.

His leading foot probed the darkness and found nothing. Muscles quivering, Blaine pulled back against the inner wall. A portion of the trail had been eaten away.

He peered down. The hollow between the granite peaks had become a bottomless chasm, a black hole whose features were indistinguishable.

But the track couldn't end here. Seevers had gone on.

Kneeling, Blaine studied the way just ahead. The ledge reappeared about six feet away, at its normal width, which was about two feet, wide enough for one man to follow it easily, or two men to sidle past each other if they were careful and neither was very fat. Long ago a portion of the ledge had crumbled. About two feet out a small, protruding lip remained. Beyond that the path had almost completely disappeared.

Close study suggested that there remained a strip of ledge perhaps three or four inches wide past the jutting lip. If that strip was solid, and if a man didn't look down or lose his nerve, he might be able to inch across.

He would be vulnerable then, helpless to defend himself or to dodge a bullet from the darkness farther down the trail.

Staring down again, his eyes plumbing the darkness a little better, Blaine saw a pale strip below, about twenty feet down. The trail was a switchback here, cutting back and forth across the steep face of the cliff.

Again he peered into the darkness ahead. He listened as intently as he stared. Every sense was alert. Sometimes you could *feel* danger present even when you could see or hear nothing. The sense of danger close by was sharp and clear, all right, but imagination would create that anyway.

With a shrug of impatience over his caution, Blaine tested the protruding lip with the toe of his boot. It seemed firm. He stepped onto it.

His back to the wall, he began to shuffle along the tiny strip of ledge that had not disintegrated. A couple of small rocks were dislodged, and he stood motionless, heart hammering loudly. He listened to the rattle of the pebbles down the sheer precipice until the sounds died away. He wondered if Lem Seevers was listening.

He also wondered how long it had taken Seevers to summon up the nerve to make this crossing.

The strip of ledge petered out. A gap of more than two feet loomed. It looked wider. Not much of a step in the ordinary way, but here Blaine would have to make it while awkwardly balanced, his weight tilted toward the wall, his back foot lacking a firm grip from which to shove.

He resisted the impulse to look down.

As he made the jump his rear foot slipped. His step fell short, barely reaching the broken edge of the path. He teetered on that edge, his arms windmilling for balance. Then one hand grabbed a projecting shoulder and pulled him forward. He stumbled safely onto the path.

Crouching on the ledge, Blaine waited for his breathing to slow and for a cramp in his left leg to ease. He was surprised that Seevers had faced up to that dangerous jump. It had taken something out of him; any such test of nerve exacted its toll. He would have guessed that it cost Seevers more, but that assessment seemed less certain now. He might have to change the judgment he had formed of Seevers during the recent weeks of the chase.

Or it might be that it was a mistake to underestimate the lengths to which fear might push a jittery man.

Whatever the impulse, Seevers had gone on. Blaine would follow. Into hell, if that was where the trail led.

The minutes pulsed by as Blaine worked his way slowly along the worn path, which doubled back and forth as it dropped down the hillside. He stopped frequently to listen, but he did not find Seevers waiting, or any sign of him. The wall of the granite ridge on the far side of the chasm moved closer as the trail wound toward the bottom. Here and there

Blaine had to feel his way over decayed sections of the path, sometimes trusting uncertain footholds that threatened to give way.

Then, unexpectedly, he came to a bridge.

It was a natural stone arch that spanned the gorge, whose lower depths remained invisible in the darkness. On the far side of the bridge the trail turned upward, climbing the steep ridge.

The feeling Blaine had been waiting for came to him as he studied the arch of rock. Somewhere on the path ahead, part way up the ridge, Seevers was waiting. He had chosen to make his stand where he could look down upon the trail rather than defend against a man above him. That eastern wall also caught a little more light. Seevers would be able to see him coming.

Peering upward, Blaine suddenly realized that a great section of the cliff far above was completely sheer. A slide or split in that face had wiped the trail away completely.

Seevers was trapped.

Blaine started across the bridge. Its surface was broken and he had to watch his footing. His boot slipped more than once on smooth rock. He wished that it were lighter, so that he could see if any other track led down into the canyon or elsewhere into the granite hills. If there were, and Seevers had stumbled onto it, he might slip away.

But in the darkness there was only one pathway visible. Moreover, the prickly feeling that Seevers was not far away persisted.

Blaine reached the far side of the natural arch without incident. He started cautiously up the trail. It twisted back on itself quickly, in places so steep that he had to use hands

as well as feet to climb. Then the switchback loops length-
ened and he was able to ascend more rapidly. He wondered
how far away that big slide was.

Then he came to another small break, five feet across.

No wonder the men of Price's Landing considered this
route impassable now, he thought.

He went down on his haunches to study the break. He
didn't like it. He couldn't see any strip of ledge remaining
that was wide enough to enable him to creep across the
gap. Had Seevers made it in one jump? In the dark?

Blaine felt another prickle of warning that made the
gooseflesh rise. Something caused him to look up. He saw
what appeared to be a setback in the wall a few feet above
his head—close enough to reach if he jumped.

Too late he realized that the trail had switched back
again. It was possible to climb to the ledge above without
having to jump the break he had reached.

In that instant he knew that Seevers had climbed that
way.

And he heard the low rumbling of a rock slide.

It was upon him before he could move. A pile of rocks
crashed down the steep hillside with the rising roar of a
flash flood slamming through a canyon. Instinctively
Blaine ducked, but it was not this that temporarily saved
his life. Most of the rocks piled into the ledge a few feet
over his head and bounced outward. He might have been
inside a waterfall. Most of the fall spilled out beyond him.
But this wasn't a rain of water, and not all of it missed him.

Smaller pebbles rained over his head and shoulders and
back, cutting and bruising his flesh. He felt a big rock
glance off his back with a force that knocked the breath

from his body. It drove him to his knees. He was dazed, engulfed in the pounding fury of the slide.

Something plucked at his shoulder and blew him off the ledge.

Battered and breathless, Blaine lay half buried. His back felt as if it must surely be broken. When he tried to move, he was convinced of it. Not only from the pain, but because he was immobilized.

The voice seemed to come from far away, and it was a while before his brain made any sense of what he heard.

"Blaine? How do you like it, Blaine? How do you like it now?" The taunt was a shriek, shrill, exultant, triumphant. "I'm here, Blaine! Why ain't you comin'? Come on, you son of a bitch, there's more! I'm gonna bury you, Blaine. I'm gonna bury you so deep you'll have to go up to get to hell!"

Blaine heard another fall start down the mountain, but it missed him. There was the thunder of the avalanche, the punishing mass of sound, a swirling curtain of dust that choked him, but he felt nothing else. The body of the slide passed several feet to his right. He could feel the bigger rocks jarring the ledge on which he lay, but that was all.

Only then did he realize that he was on a portion of the trail.

His mind was functioning very slowly. In its plodding way it told him what had happened. The first slide of rocks had knocked him off the ledge now immediately above him. The trail, switching back, had caught him at the next level, after most of the torrent of stone had passed over him. In falling he must have been knocked to one side, and the second slide had missed him completely.

He tried to move again. Sweat broke out on his forehead. From the waist down he was securely pinned under a pile of debris. From the pain in one leg he guessed that an ankle or other bone was broken. But some small rocks shifted when he made the effort to move, and he felt life in one arm.

He wasn't dead. He wasn't completely paralyzed. He wasn't even through fighting.

Blaine forced himself to think of Samantha, releasing the searing vision that he usually tried to keep caged. It was a kind of self-flagellation, and the hot, vivid sting of that memory spurred him into new tests of his battered body, shifting his shoulders and freeing his right arm.

He heard Lem Seevers' voice again, closer, clearer. He groped for the Colt Shaughnessy had given him. He knew he hadn't lost it. He had stuffed it under his waistband, and he could feel the hard shape of the gun digging into his belly.

"Blaine? Say something, damn you! Tell me what you're gonna do to me now, you hairy reptile. I'm listenin'. You don't talk so loud no more. I don't hear any of them rattles. Hell, I heered you was so tough I should ride around you like you was a swamp." Seevers laughed wildly, delighted with himself. "Damn, I did it! Me! Lem Seevers! Not ol' Abe Stillwell. Not Ned Keatch, neither. You din't even know ol' Ned was in on it, did you, Blaine? Or did Abe tell you about that Keatch? Why, he was second on, Blaine. He couldn't hardly wait for Abe to climb off before he jumped in. Wait'll he hears what Lem Seevers done for him. Wait'll all those bold, bad demons hears. Wait'll I tell 'em!"

Ned Keatch, Blaine thought without surprise. His name hadn't come up before. No one had known that that quick-draw gambler was running with the Clancy boys.

Ned Keatch. Gunfighter. Faro artist. Rapist and murderer. A new name to remember. A new face to search for. A new reason for Cullom Blaine to stay alive.

Blaine felt sharp pain in his chest when he fumbled across his ribs for the single-action Colt. A cracked rib, most likely. He ignored the pain, found the well-worn butt of the six gun, tugged it loose. He tried not to dislodge any of the slide debris that covered him. He managed to slip the gun free of his waistband, but he had to stop there. He couldn't pull it clear without rattling some rocks and warning Seevers that he was still alive.

"Where are you, Blaine? In hell?"

In his glee Seevers jumped up and down. Dust filtered over the side of the ledge where he danced. Blaine felt the fine spray on his face.

He was backed up against the wall so that he was more or less in a sitting position, hidden in shadow, his legs projecting across the ledge. Little of him showed clearly. The coating over his torso was mostly dust and small gravel. A heavier pile pinned down his legs, and one boot protruded from that pile, sticking out beyond the edge of the trail.

Peering down from the ledge above, Lem Seevers made out that one boot in the dim light. He shrieked with delight. "You still wearin' your boots, Blaine? I figgered you'd of jumped right out of 'em." Seevers cackled at his own humor. Everything cheered him now. "Let's see if you're still kickin'."

Seevers took quick aim and fired into the darkness

below. His first shot missed. With the second he saw the protruding boot jerk from the impact as a bullet passed through the toe. There was nothing but that reflex bounce, however, apparently confirming that there was no life inside the boot or in the body to which it was connected. Seevers laughed so hard that he fell down and rolled on the ledge.

Cullom Blaine cut his tongue trying to bite off a yell. Seevers' bullet had hit a toe. He stared at his foot through watery eyes. The reason it wasn't jumping and kicking was the fact that his legs were both buried, and that left leg was quite probably broken. That lead-burned left foot was flopped over at an odd angle.

Seevers rose, chortling and hallooing. Blaine heard him start along the ledge, trotting, no longer concerned about making noise. And of a sudden Blaine knew that that broken bone in his leg had saved his life.

He waited until Seevers had moved down the line some distance. He was heading for the next turn in the trail that would bring him back on the lower level. When Blaine thought he heard Seevers turning back he risked his move.

He dragged the borrowed Colt clear.

Waiting, Blaine felt none of the gleeful satisfaction that had seized Lem Seevers. He felt old pain and new, and behind that only the weariness of a man who has come to the end of one leg of a long journey.

He shook the gun, which was covered with dust, and thumbed back the hammer. He hoped that the dust and gravel had not damaged the gun.

He could hear the sound of Seevers' footsteps approaching along the path. Then the man himself appeared in outline. When Seevers was less than twenty feet away he let out another delighted yip, seeing the rock pile blocking the trail, marked by that single protruding boot.

"Yippee! You still there, you catamount? Can't hear you spit. Ain't you got nothin' to say?"

"Talk's done," Blaine said.

He squeezed the trigger—and the Colt misfired.

Lem Seevers heard the loud slam of the hammer on a dud cartridge, and the low voice coming from the shadowy pile. His breath caught and he whispered, "Oh, Jesus," and jerked his own gun up.

Blaine's Colt kicked in his hand with the second shot, and Lem Seevers' body bucked as the bullet struck him high on the chest. It flopped him around. He bounced off the slanting wall. Still on his feet, he floundered backward. His gun exploded from a reflex squeeze of his finger, the muzzle pointing down. Blaine's next bullet ripped across Seevers' buttocks. By then he was already toppling off the ledge, and the last shot intended for him went high.

Blaine heard the body flopping down the steep hillside. It started up another small avalanche.

# TWENTY-ONE

Shaughnessy and three others from Price's Landing found Cullom Blaine on the ledge the next morning. They had been stopped once in their search by the break in the western slope, and one man had returned to the camp for a couple of long, stout planks. One of the boards made a bridge over the fall. The other became a stretcher on which

Blaine was carried back to the Landing.

Lem Seevers was found dead in the bottom of the gorge, where he was left.

Blaine was kept under guard in Price's Landing. His various cuts and skin scrapings were cleaned out with whisky, and the deep cut in his left arm from Sam Price's knife was cauterized with a hot iron. An old-timer familiar with broken bones straightened out Blaine's leg and made a rude wooden splint for it to keep the cracked ankle rigid while it mended. Otherwise Blaine was bruised and battered all over, but he would heal. His broken rib, if that's what it was, didn't seem to be poking into anything; it would take care of itself. Until it did he would have to breathe shallow, that was all.

"We got to get you out of here," Shaughnessy told him, confirming that Sam Price had died from his belly wound. "Can't answer for what'll happen if we tries to keep you for long."

An uneasy truce had been struck between those who wanted to avenge Price and those who believed that fair play demanded Blaine's safe release. The fuse had burned right down to the dynamite the night of the fight. The little bank teller, whose full name was Clement Mordecai Early, had nipped it off.

"Early just kind of took over," Shaughnessy said, shaking his head in wonder. "Shows you can't always rate a bull by the length of his horns. The little feller made everyone see that we had to pull together or Price's Landing was gonna go up in smoke. It's gonna be different. That Early can't run things like Sam did. It'll be the council that has the say. But Early says that's the way it oughta be.

197

He's right, ain't he, Blaine?"

"I reckon he is."

Early had also sent scouts out as far as McAlister's valley, and at the end of Blaine's third day of recuperation the word came back that J. P. Holifield's siege of the camp had been lifted, just as Blaine had claimed. That confirmation changed the mood of the camp somewhat, bringing more men over to Blaine's side. Sam Price, after all, had been planted. After anger cooled, reasonable heads argued that Price's Landing could go on without him, but not if it was a house divided over Blaine. A full meeting of the council ruled unanimously that Blaine should be escorted safely from the camp as soon as he was able to ride. In the meanwhile there would be no reprisal—an order that carried the full weight of the newly invigorated council's authority.

By the fifth day Blaine was feeling close to normal, and able to hobble on his wooden splint with the help of a cane. He spent some time that afternoon accustoming Randy to the idea that he would be mounting the buckskin from the right side. Blaine could carry only one foot in the stirrup, but he thought he could stay in the saddle.

The next morning he left Price's Landing. He didn't ride down the canyon alone. Several others were anxious to leave the camp behind, now that the way was clear. One rider was heading north, by way of McAlister's ranch, and he suggested that Blaine might accompany him there. He would be able to rest a while at the ranch.

Blaine thought of Iris McAlister. "No," he said. The prospect was too tempting.

Three other men were riding west to the Pecos and

beyond. Blaine went with them as far south as the Middle Concho and the old Emigrant Route west. There the three outlaws were to follow the sun, and Blaine left them.

He would be safer west of the Pecos. Going east meant that he might have to spend much of his time lying in the willows and watering at night, for he didn't believe that J. P. Holifield would forgive or forget, and a drifter called Blaine might soon be a target for every man with a badge in Texas.

But his search wasn't over.

He would ride the high line now, alone, but that didn't matter to him. It had just happened that way without his choosing. It wouldn't stop him. Nothing would.

The men who rode west to the Pecos carried Blaine's story with them, exaggerating it a little with each telling, as men do around a campfire. That was how the legend began to grow.

**Center Point Publishing**
600 Brooks Road ● PO Box 1
Thorndike ME 04986-0001 USA

(207) 568-3717

US & Canada:
1 800 929-9108